D-TOURS

D-TOURS

a
novel by
Jonathan Baumbach

Normal

Published by FC2 with support given by the English
Department Unit for Contemporary Literature of
Illinois State University, and the Illinois Arts Council.

Address all inquiries to:
FC2, Unit for Contemporary Literature
Illinois State University, Campus Box 4241
Normal, IL 61790-4241.

ISBN: Paper, 1-57366-037-X, $12.95

Library of Congress Cataloging-in-Publication Data
Baumbach, Jonathan 1938–
        D-tours : a novel / by Jonathan Baumbach. — 1st ed.
            p.   cm.
        ISBN 157366-037-X (alk. paper)
        I. Title.
PS3552.A844D8   1998
813' .54—dc21   98–13870
                                                         CIP

Book Design: Brian Monday
Cover Design: Todd Michael Bushman
Cover Photographs: David Axel Baumbach

Produced and printed in the United States of America

Illinois
ARTS
Council
AN AGENCY OF
THE STATE OF ILLINOIS

This program is
partially sponsored
by a grant from the
Illinois Arts Council

For my son, David, whose photographic
series, "Stills From Imaginary Movies,"
inspired this novel.

...the very dreams that blister
sleep, boil up from the basic
magic ring of myth.

—Joseph Campbell,
The Hero With a Thousand Faces

preface

They say, whoever, that life imitates the movies. (Clichés for all their bad report tend to get it mostly right.) My life, as you'll see, has been a movie, or fifty movies. Though a late starter, I've run a gamut of careers in my time from private detective to screenwriter to secret agent to transactional therapist to CEO to intergalactic traveler to deranged visionary, you name it. It's all on my resume, though not always under the same name. Currently, I am in the fugitive business, employed as you might imagine by desperation rather than choice. My job as fugitive is to keep moving without leaving tracks, a late-life career for which I am in a certain sense overqualified.

You catch me at the moment in an out-of-the-way motel somewhere in North Dakota run by a taxidermist with shifty eyes. By the time you read this, I'll be somewhere else or nowhere at all.

If only I hadn't gotten up from my table in the Russian Tea Room to make a phone call at a most unpropitious moment, I might have gone on as I had, living the good life, producing motion pictures, losing my heart with reckless abandon to seductive, unavailable, heartbreaking women.

Making movies was what I had always wanted to do, but as you will see when you hear my story, I had taken more than a few detours before finding my way to the heart's port of call.

I had set up as an independent producer in Los Angeles (with a presence in New York), one of the so-called new breed, making audience-friendly pictures of a not everyday nature, showcasing new and distinctive talent, telling the stories my pollsters told me needed to be told. I had just nurtured two quality films, and I was in preproduction on a third, when I made the fatal error of getting up from my table to phone Lola.

I was always a soupçon hyperactive; I could never stay in one place for long. The story of my life is the story of how I ran from career to career, leaving traces of myself everywhere. I was like a dog chasing its own tail, except I was the tail and the chaser, both at once. All the stuff they warn you about is true: you reap what you sow, you get what you pay for, loss is the ultimate effect of the cause of having.

This was how it happened. I had just accessed a valuable property over dinner at the Russian Tea Room, and I got up from my table on unexamined impulse to call Lola, a former wife I had not talked to in years. I got up from my table to make a phone call that had suddenly seemed an inescapable necessity at the very moment some duplicitous international agent was being paged by the people hoping to trap him. Once I was mistaken for this ostensibly dangerous figure, a man of a thousand faces, my life was fatefully altered. Detours tend to be irrevocable or tend to be the trip you meant to take all along. What happened to me at the end was different only in kind from the scenarios that preceded it.

I have this theory that nothing you do is real unless others know about it—the more others, as I see it, the more real—and continue to know about it, and continue to dream about it, and remember it as if your experiences were also theirs. So in a sense you've been on this trip with me, though the news hasn't quite reached you yet. You'll wake up one morning, and it will be all there down to the last detail.

Whatever the authorities may say about me, I am no more guilty of their random charges than you are. The experts say that defensiveness invites disbelief. So I'm not asking you to take my word, merely to hear me out. My sense of innocence has never been so finely tuned.

What follows is the scenario of my several careers on and off the silver screen and the circumstantial events that connected them. I only hope—it is all I ask at the moment—

that those who are committed to running me down will not succeed in their quest until the complete story is told.

The whole of it, inevitably, is truer than the sum of its amazements. The adventure started innocently enough. I got up from my table at the Russian Tea Room on a whim—my meal half-finished—to make a phone call.

part 1

one

When I was forced to leave Hollywood, I was determined that it would be a temporary detour at worst. Still, it would take me fifteen years and a handful of other abortive careers before I returned to filmmaking, one misadventure inspiring another.

Semi-fatal love was my perpetual unmooring. When I fell, when I lost my heart, I seemed to fall headlong and forever. I fell hard, and when I got back on my feet, I was never quite the same person again.

Am I getting ahead of myself here, rushing off with unseemly haste to the final fade to black? Maybe it wasn't love at all, but chance, blind circumstance, fate, that kept me away for the longest time from what I wanted most to do.

Maybe what I did was take the wrong flight or get seated next to the wrong woman on the wrong flight. Exiled from Hollywood, I had gone into the public relations business in San Francisco (a psychotherapy student at Stanford in my spare time), and I was returning from an assignment in Paris, which had led me also to Brussels, Milan and Beirut, causing the postponement of my return for almost a month. Everything factored in to this chance meeting. And even if I knew in advance what was going to happen, I would have accepted my ultimately unhappy fate with open arms.

I was aware when I took my seat in business class that there was an attractive Eurasian woman at the window seat next to me, but I had other things on my mind. And she too seemed preoccupied. Absorbed in the book she was reading— it was *The Lover* by Marguerite Duras—she paid virtually no attention to my arrival. For the first two hours of our trip, we conspicuously ignored each other, barely exchanged a word. Our willful avoidance of one another was probably a telltale sign.

Sudden turbulence, which caused our plane to freefall a few thousand feet before righting itself, created the occasion for conversation between us. We talked about the times in our lives when we felt ourselves in danger. It was a subject that opened up feelings of vulnerability, a subject which forced intimacy upon us whether we were looking for it or not.

Her name was Marisan, and before the flight was over, I was hopelessly in love with her. I sensed she liked me some, but I had no idea that she reciprocated my feelings with the same violent intensity.

We had an overnight stop in New York, and I suggested we meet for dinner for which she thanked me with a sad smile, saying it wasn't possible. Much as she would like it to be, it simply wasn't. She was married to a good man; she didn't philander. I too was married at the moment—it was to the actress (and anthropologist) Lola Monet—but we had not been living together (not living living together) for some time. What happened between us on the flight, what was continuing to happen, even while we chattered on as if we had known each other all our lives, could never be anything more than a seductively elusive encounter.

We were silent for awhile, the plane descending, preparing itself to land, when she said rather fiercely, her thoughts seeming to speak themselves, "I owe my life to him, my husband. He's a wonderful doctor, a world-famous heart specialist. Do you understand?"

What I understood was that she was confessing her feelings for me by warning me of her commitment to her husband. It was enough to know that she loved me, it made renunciation possible, it made never seeing her again bearable. We went our separate ways without saying goodbye, and I let the crowd part us because I was with her, went with her even as I remained behind, observing from a distance her unselfconscious grace as she hailed a cab. I might have ordered the next cab in line to follow her, but I didn't need to. I knew the name of her hotel.

I had to wait two hours for her to emerge, and when she did, I made no effort to disguise my presence. Though she knew I was there, she gave no sign of acknowledgment, neither of pleasure nor displeasure. She merely went on in her unhurried pace, passing like some unearned grace through the city, to Chelsea to the Village to Soho to the lower east side, following some private blueprint, and I followed about ten steps behind, glancing at her only to make sure she was still there. We shared the city, observed the same passing scene, a time lag of approximately five seconds separating us.

It was August and the city was overrun with tourists. The same shops passed us, the same restaurants, the same theaters, the same coteries of Japanese, the same overweight German couple holding a white-haired child between them—the child sporting a button with a swastika on it—the same ratty prostitutes, the same violent street gangs. We must have walked five miles in the same manner, separated by no more than ten steps. She must have known I was following her and yet she never looked back. At some point—perhaps I was testing her intentions—I turned around and went the other way. I let a few blocks pass before glancing back, and there she was, a glow in the shadows, walking along some ten steps behind me, her eyes on the ground.

Then during a police action, trapped briefly in a crowd of looters and German tourists, we lost each other. Or perhaps she had gone on to something else. I retraced my steps, walked back and forth, returning each time to where I had lost her, the spot becoming a shrine to my despair. It was 2 AM, and when I saw a cab coming, I moved to hail it. Through the windows of the cab, as it sped by me, I saw Marisan across the street, frail and panicked, looking in all directions. I ran toward her, calling her name, and she waited for me, arms outstretched.

Without a word of explanation, we walked, no longer in single file, to the nearest lodging, a flea-bag called The Paradise Hotel, and I asked for their best room, which had nothing to recommend it beyond a soot-fogged window and a broken air conditioner. Then we undressed each other in what seemed like slow motion and got under the covers and fell asleep in each other's arms. In the morning, in a pace so deliberate we seemed barely to be moving, we made love for the first time, and an hour later, for the second. Then we talked about our worst faults and fell asleep again, not waking until it was night outside. Then we began to talk again, Marisan asking about my childhood, and we agreed to exchange stories. I told her about this murder I witnessed from my bedroom window when I was seven.

We were living in the Midwest at the time, in the heartland of the country, across the road from a public golf course which I thought of as my own private magic carpet. I loved to watch the balls arrive mysteriously on the green like wingless birds from another world until this traumatic thing happened that ruined the game of golf for me forever. I had been sent to my room for telling stories and was lying in bed gawking out the window, the course fogged-in, a mucky drizzle impeding play. I was staring out the window in my dreamy way when I noticed two men on the 15th green leaning into each other, whispering secrets. It was like watching TV with the sound off. The smaller one, who looked like the cartoon figure Popeye, was making these wild gestures and the other, a bulky guy in a green parka, responded by hitting him repeatedly across the side of the head with a golf club. I had never knowingly witnessed violence before, and I imagined I was watching an aspect of golf that made sense only to those who knew all the rules. At some point, the smaller guy collapsed to the green, face down, like a shadow, the man in the parka glancing around him to see if anyone had been watching. After awhile, he fixed on my cherubic face pressed like a moon to the window.

Frightened by his crazed stare, I fled from the room and told my mother what I had witnessed, improving on the truth only for the sake of a better story, and though she didn't quite believe me, didn't know what to believe, she phoned the police. When the men in blue got around to checking out the 15th green, the body of the fallen man was gone. It was assumed that I had been dreaming or had made up the story to attract attention. I had a reputation for having an overheated imagination, so when my father came home and was briefed on my disgrace, I was exiled to my room. Before they would allow me my freedom, I had to promise never to tell stories again. Everyone seemed so certain that I had imagined the unimaginable that I was almost ready to believe it myself, except I had occasion a few days later to see the man in the

green parka a second time. Mother had a doctor's appointment, so father took me with him to his office, and while I
was goofing at his desk, his boss came in to discuss some business with him. Standing in front of me in a double-breasted
blue suit was the man in the green parka. Recognition between
us was immediate on my part, delayed on his. The shocked
look on my face must have given me away, must have con-
firmed him in his suspicion that I was the face he had seen
framed in the window.

On the way home I asked my father if he liked his boss,
and he said the man was like a god, so I knew I couldn't tell
him the truth without disappointing him in me further. You
see, my tarnished reputation had irrevocably damaged my credibility. And that, as you can see, wasn't the worst of my
problem. The worst of it was that a murderer knew I had witnessed his crime.

The next day when I got out of school, the boss appeared
out front in this fancy black car and said he was there to pick
me up as a favor to my father. I ran away, but he was able to
trail alongside me in his car, telling me not to be silly, repeating the phrase "no need to be silly" over and over. When I saw
a police officer directing traffic, I dodged over to him and
said this man I had seen commit a murder was following me
in his car. The cop pulled the boss over, and they talked for
awhile out of my hearing. Then the cop came over and said to
me "Kid, you better get in that car and not cause any more
trouble." He had me by the wrist so I couldn't run away.

I knew, once I was in the car and we were driving in a
direction I had never been before, that the boss meant to get
rid of me forever. I said to him, "If you let me go, I promise I
won't tell anyone. Besides no one believes anything I say. They
think I make things up just to get attention."

He pretended not to know what I was talking about, said
he was taking me to see my father. I told him just take me
home, and he kept saying, "Sure, kid," and the next thing I
knew we're walking along this cliff in the country, and he's
dragging me by the arm. I offered no resistance, which put
him off his guard, and then when he relaxed his grip, I broke
away. It all happened so quickly after that it's hard to pinpoint
the sequence in memory. I remember backing to the edge of
the cliff to avoid being grabbed, putting myself in the most
vulnerable situation, the boss stalking me. He was out of breath,

his breathing like some nightmare sound. All of a sudden he lunged at me, I dodged, and he fell over.

When I finally got home, and I told my father his boss tried to kidnap me—I was at a loss for an explanation for my belated return—he sent me to my room. "I don't want to hear another story from you ever again," he said.

I thought when the boss's body was found, they would blame me for the murder, but they never did. A few days later, I heard my father tell my mother that his boss had died in a suspicious accident. "Do you see?" I wanted to say to them, but I was afraid I would get in trouble if I admitted what I had done. You're the first one I ever told, I said to Marisan.

"How terrible for you," she said, tears running down her face.

Then she told me her story, which was more terrible still.

two

At nine, in a rural town in France—Marisan had a French father and a Vietnamese mother—her voices (as she called them) spoke to her for the first time. Her mother, who confused mysticism with willfulness, locked her in a wine cellar as punishment for insisting that she had otherworldly advisors. In isolation, her voices were even more in evidence, whispering to her, "Pick up your stick, it will go," which was not something she understood until much later on. She assumed the voices were advising her to use a stick to beat off the boys at school who tended to tease her about her Asian eyes.

One day, she went to the local priest, an amiable drunkard, to ask him if her voices came from God. The priest was encouraging, said that Marisan may have been chosen by God for a special destiny, but behind her back he told her parents that she was indulging herself in fantasy. Her stepfather, who was a well-meaning brute, beat her in an attempt to bring her in contact with reality. Reality in that family came in blows.

Years passed without further word from her voices, and she missed them, felt abandoned by their absence. Big for her age, she tended to get in trouble at school for fighting with the boys. One time when she was locked in the basement of the school for kicking a foul-mouthed boy, the voices mysteriously returned. It was the same incomprehensible message:

"Pick up your stick, it will go," they whispered. When she confided to her parents that her voices had returned, they sent her away to a home for Wayward Girls and Presumptive Visionaries, a one-of-a-kind place just outside Lyon. She would have been miserable there except that her voices kept her company, offered solace and prophesy, though the particulars of the message remained obscure. "I have reason to believe that I have a special destiny," she told the therapist at the Home, "though besides beating boys with a stick, I don't know what I'm supposed to do."

The therapist was as duplicitous as the priest. He pretended to be her ally, told her she was one of God's children, then under the pretext of getting closer to God, he deflowered her. When Marisan protested, the therapist told the security guards she was dangerous and had them lock her in her room.

Psychically wounded by her betrayal, in a near-suicidal funk, she escaped from the Home by taking the advice of her voices who were at that point chattering incessantly. "Take the turn, avoid the burn," they told her.

It wasn't as if Marisan had any place to go. When she escaped from the Wayward Home, she returned to her parents, who agreed to hide her from the authorities if she promised not to mention the voices in their presence. When those who would take her away came to get her—at this point they were saying she was a dangerously crazy person, a thief and a murderer—her mother disguised her as a boy and locked her in the basement. After a while, still disguised as a boy, she began to leave the house again.

A barnstorming team of American baseball players came to her town and, having nothing better to do, Marisan, in her guise as a farmboy, went to the game which was played at a local football pitch. Then an odd thing happened that changed the course of her life. In each of the games the barnstorming team played, someone was invited from the audience to pinch-hit in the ninth inning. Her number was called, and she reluctantly left the makeshift stands to bat with the bases loaded in the home team's last at bat. Now she had never held a bat in her hands before, but it seemed the most natural thing in the world. On the third pitch, she introduced the bat to the ball and watched the horsehide sail over the centerfielder's head for a homerun. Rounding the bases with the encouragement of the other players (surrounded by cheering), she had a revelation.

This was what her voices meant when they said, "Pick up your stick, it will go." She had; it did. The manager of the barnstorming team took her aside afterward and told her she was a natural. He then invited her to join them on the tour and maybe even go to America with them afterward.

She locked herself in the basement that night to get counsel from her voices who were encouraging in their cryptic way. The next morning she said goodbye to her parents (who despite the trouble she had caused were sad to see her leave), and she went off on the barnstorming tour with the American players. She toured France for a while, coming out of the stands in boy's disguise to hit homeruns in Aix, Montpelier and Perigord. At long last, she was pursuing the calling her voices had chosen for her.

Known as "Frenchy," she made her debut in organized baseball with the Class A Ottawa Owls. After only two weeks of play, she was advanced to Double A and joined the Ronkonkoma Railbirds, who were mired in the basement on her arrival. Saddened by her team's failure, she told the manager, a dour man named Grumpy Harris, in her as yet unformed English, that she was destined to bring fortune to his team.

It was the wrong thing to say and the manager punished her for her presumption by keeping her on the bench. A month went by before she got the chance to redeem herself. The regular left-fielder, who suffered from bouts of disequilibrium, hit his head against a wall chasing an unexceptional fly ball. He was carried off the field, mumbling to himself in a dazed state that he would catch the ball in a moment if the others gave him room. As no one else was available, Marisan was put in the game as the substitute left-fielder.

In her first chance in the outfield—her voices sent her in the wrong direction in what she took to be a private joke—she badly misplayed a fly ball and was hooted by the fans. In her first at bat, with two strikes against her, and two runners on, she hit an opposite field homerun. After that, she was in the line-up without exception every day and was a great favorite in her adoptive hometown, but of course no one knew she was an imposter.

In two months time, she helped the Railbirds move from last place to second, a handful of percentage points from first. So as not to give her true sex away, she didn't shower or dress with the other players, claiming a sacred French-Vietnamese tradition against undressing with strangers in the room. She supposed this made her something of a mystery, and the point of mysteries was to solve them. Obnoxious reporters followed her after the game, looking to discover something revealing about her that would make their reputations. When they didn't find anything—she had no life beyond the game—they made up stories, said she was the illegitimate son of a famous blind Japanese samurai. One paper said she was a miracle man and had healed a sore-armed pitcher merely by touching him on the shoulder.

Each day a new outlandish story about her secret past headlined the back pages of the local tabloids. One paper had it that she had once spent six months in a home for wayward girls, which made her anxious when it appeared. Still, it was not a story that anyone wanted to believe.

In the last week of the season, the Railbirds beat their major rivals, the Durham Bulls, two games out of three to put them in a nose-to-nose tie for first. A playoff game was arranged, winner take all, and then fate played her a bitter trick. The night before the playoff game, she ate something that didn't agree with her, or perhaps, as was conjectured in the press, someone had poisoned her—she was known to have enemies. In any event, she found herself in the hospital, running a high fever, too weak even to get out of bed.

The Railbirds were down two runs in the fourth inning when she begged the doctor to give her something that would permit her to play. "I could do that," he said—he was a brilliant doctor, the man she would one day marry—"but it could be extremely dangerous. The likelihood is, you would never play another game of baseball if you played this one." She said the risks didn't concern her; winning this game was the only thing that mattered.

So the doctor gave her this experimental drug which took away her pain and fever for three hours, and she rushed to the ball park. When she got there, the Railbirds were three runs behind in the seventh inning and everyone, even Grumpy Harris, seemed overjoyed to see her. In the eighth inning, her team had runners on first and second with one out, and Harris sent her in to pinch hit. All her depleted energies were focused on hitting a home run, but the pitcher, recognizing the danger, walked her intentionally, which flew in the face of conventional baseball wisdom. Her teammates got two of the runners in, and the Railbirds came into the ninth inning only one run down.

She thought her opportunity for heroics was over, but in the ninth inning the Railbirds loaded the bases with two outs, and she had a second chance.

The Bulls brought their ace pitcher in to face her, and she knew he had been overworked and was almost as tired as she was. Her voices advised her to take the first three pitches, all of which were balls. The fourth pitch the ace threw her was the one she was looking for, a hanging slider. She punished it with her best swing, and then she stood at home plate watching it sail toward the stands, barely able to control her happiness. At the last minute, the Bulls' centerfielder, who would someday be a famous major leaguer (though would die in an airplane crash at the height of his powers), made an impossible leap and caught the ball, his arm extended beyond the fence.

Marisan collapsed from the disappointment, and when the medics tried to revive her, they discovered that she was a woman and an imposter. As punishment, the authorities banned her from the game (deleting her records from the books) forever. Shortly after that, she married the doctor who had saved her life, and her voices never spoke to her again.

three

There was more to Marisan's story. As a consequence of taking the drug that had made it possible for her to play the last few innings of the biggest game of her life, she had developed an incurable heart condition that meant each day she survived was borrowed time. She had been living with her death sentence for six years, living each day as if it were her last. And her husband, who was a brilliant doctor, could do nothing more than ease her pain. He was powerless to save her. "So you see," she said, "our love is doomed one way or another."

"I will stay with you to the end," I said, barely able to speak. "I will never leave your side."

Sitting up in bed, she reminded me that there were other people in our lives to consider, her husband and my estranged wife, our employers and co-workers, not to mention society itself which was dependent for its survival on its collective beliefs. "Isn't it enough that we've had this day together?" she said. "To ask for the sun when you've had the moon and stars must surely seem ungrateful."

I conceded her point and said that I would walk out of her life in a few minutes, that it would take me a little time to work up the courage, but that was only talk. My intent was to distract her. I was, with all good will, incapable of walking out the door.

I told her another story, extended our time together for as long as I could.

I woke up on the morning of my sixteenth birthday, my story started, with my life in disarray. My parents were negotiating a divorce, my sister was having an affair with my stepfather's older brother, hyperactive Uncle Al, and the girl I loved (and as yet hadn't spoken to) was the announced property of the captain of the football team, a mean-spirited arrogant bully named Ace, who was also the second richest kid in our provincial Michigan town. And to top off the bad news, no one seemed to have a clue that today was my birthday.

No one that is except my best pal Sassy (her real name was Miriam) who, though female and pretty enough when she cleaned up and made the effort, hung out with us as if she were one of the guys. You could always confide your problems to Sassy, who had an optimistic nature and was generous with advice. "Don't get down on yourself, Fret," she said—everyone called me Fret that year—"your folks are probably into the surprise party thing and are just letting you think they've forsaken you so as not to spoil the surprise." I didn't know that then, but Sassy had a secret crush on me and would have died of embarrassment if it ever got out.

Anyway, we were talking in her room when she gave me a goof birthday gift to cheer me up, a pair of hand-knitted socks, each almost big enough to put both feet in at the same time. Sassy would always give you some kind of funny present to make you laugh. That's when I told her about Euphoria, the girl I had been out of my mind in love with for almost a week. It grieved her when I sang Euphoria's praises, but she never let on aside from an almost unnoticeable tic in her left eye. "Just be yourself when you're with her," she told me. "If you're yourself, Fret, the girl will love you for those qualities peculiar to your nature." I knew it was good advice because it was the kind of thing everyone always said to you, but in the past the only girl I'd ever been able to be myself with was Sassy.

Between classes at Riverview High, between third and fourth periods unless memory lies, I passed Euphoria in the hall, and we exchanged smiles like secret confessions. It was her smile that encouraged me to approach her. Without the usual preliminaries—I was being nothing if not myself—I asked her if she would like to go out with me on my birthday, which was the following Friday. She said, yes she would but no she couldn't because she and her boyfriend Ace had agreed not to see other people. I tried to be cool, which meant not showing her how crushed I was by her rejection, and as a consequence of holding back my feelings, I fainted at her feet. I woke to find my head in her lap, Euphoria stroking my hair. "Of course I'll go out with you on your birthday, Fret," she was saying. "No one has ever fainted for me before."

The next part is part hearsay, part conjecture. When Euphoria told Ace that she was going on a date with me on my birthday because it seemed the decent thing to do, Ace, with the aid and instigation of his sociopathic friend Summerfield, decided to teach his rival a lesson he would not soon forget. Marisan, these guys had a strong sense of entitlement and believed anything they did to further their own goals was acceptable behavior.

Anyway, when I returned home from school a little earlier than anticipated, my sister and Uncle Al were in my parents' bedroom. The heavy-breathing noises scared me, which was why I happened to open the door. "Where's mom and dad?" I asked to cover my embarrassment. "They both have appointments at their lawyers'," my sister said.

"This isn't what it looks like," said Uncle Al, who was a fidgeter. "I was just comforting your sister who's going through some hard times."

I got out of that room as fast as I could, muttering under my breath that I didn't care what they did.

A phone call came to the house from the local lock-up, somebody saying my stepfather was in jail for being drunk and disorderly. The only way I could get together the money for his bail was to pawn my second-hand tux, which was what I was planning to wear on my date. Right after his release, my stepfather made me a solemn promise that he'd never take another drink in this lifetime. It was not the first such promise he had made. Twenty minutes later, before I could get him home, he detoured into a bar.

"All you have to do is be yourself, Dad," I said, passing on Sassy's advice, and he said, "What the fuck do you think I'm doing, kid?"

I had nothing suitable to wear, and I was about to call off the date when Sassy arrived with a new tux she had spent every last cent of her savings to buy me. I told her I couldn't accept such an expensive gift, but she said it would be bad manners on my part not to accept it so I gave in, kissing my pal Sassy in unpremeditated gesture of gratitude. My mistake was to kiss her on the lips, which opened up feelings that had never bothered to announce themselves before. The next thing I knew I was lying on top of Sassy on the rug, a voice in the back of my head warning me that I would lose my best friend unless I stopped what I was doing before the situation got out of hand. So I rolled off Sassy and climbed to my feet, saying I hoped I hadn't ruined everything. While I was holding out my hand to her in apology, she slapped my face and rushed out of the house.

I would have gone after Sassy, but just then a cop came by to say my mother was in the hospital, the result of a failed suicide attempt, mom having taken an overdose of some prescription tranquilizer. I stopped off at the hospital to see my mother, who was so groggy she didn't recognize me, then I picked up Euphoria in my Chevy pick-up for our date, which I had spent a sleepless night planning to the last detail.

First stop was at the new restaurant in town called El Steak House, and that was the only part of the date we concluded. As we were about to step from the restaurant, Euphoria noticed Ace's black van in the parking lot out front, and she suggested we go out the back and make a run for it. As much as it made sense, I couldn't allow myself to run away. My self-respect, which at sixteen seemed fragile and unassailable, was firmly on the line.

When I saw that my tires had been slashed and dog urine poured over my truck, I knew I would have to fight Ace, who was about six inches and forty pounds bigger. When Ace stepped out of his van, I said, "What's the big idea?" facing him down as though I weren't afraid. At the same time, Summerfield came around from the blind side and pinned my arms. It was no fair fight. Ace punched me at will while Summerfield held me from behind. Euphoria called to them to stop, but they mocked her protests. "Stop," they said in falsetto voices, "stop, stop, stop." "You're a gutless lowlife," I remember saying to Ace, which was the last thing I said before blacking out from a brass-knuckle punch to the side of the head.

I woke with my head in Sassy's lap—at first I thought it was Euphoria—my face like hamburger, my head and body a mass of aches. When I heard a voice saying, "That was dumb, Fret," I knew whose elegant lap harbored my aching head. It was my best friend, Sassy, who always told me the unvarnished truth.

When I learned that Ace and Summerfield had kidnapped Euphoria and taken her to Summerfield's family estate, I kind of knew what I had to do. Anger focused me. My resolve was absolute.

I borrowed Sassy's car and appeared at Summerfield's parents' estate like an avenging angel, where, as in a dream, I wiped up the room with my tormentors, leaving one unconscious and the other badly shaken, cowering in a corner, a few priceless antiques smashed in the process, everything happening in dream time, my rescuing Euphoria (who was about to be gang-raped), my making love to her, which was my first time, my having to choose between the two girls and picking Sassy (for whom my feelings were more than illusion), bringing both girls to my home for temporary safekeeping, entering a dark house, tired and bleeding, strung out from my ordeal, expecting God knows what, when without warning the lights flashed on, and my family and friends appeared in the living room, Mom, stepdad, sis, Uncle Al, Aunt Gert, granny, cousin Bob, my half-brother Marco, Sassy, Euphoria, the upstairs neighbors, and they cried out to me all in one voice, "Happy Birthday, Fret," and what could I do but fall to my knees in a kind of ecstasy, my arms raised in triumph and say, "This is the happiest day of my life."

"Max, as much as I don't want to leave you, one of us should go," Marisan said. She got up from the bed as if she had already decided she would be the one.

"I'll go, Marisan," I said, taking her wrist, dissembling, "after I tell you one more story."

She lay back on the bed, pleased, it seemed, to have an excuse to stay together just a little longer. "Just one more," she said.

four

I was often in trouble when I was a kid, my next story started, had run with a nasty crowd of feckless guys. One time a girl was accidentally killed by one of our group and, though no one actually approved of the killing, the guys decided that the right thing to do was to stand by our friend no matter what. Mostly no one seemed to care that the girl was killed, an aspect probably more of denial than callousness. The guy who killed her, Ace, was out of control and not particularly likeable in ordinary circumstances. Even so, we adhered to a code of silence which the rich kids among us had learned from their dads. When Ace killed a second woman, someone who had been a friend, I broke ranks and made an anonymous phone call to the police. Ace was never arrested—he was the son of one of the town's leading citizens—but he ended up putting a bullet in his head. It was an uncharacteristic, inexplicable act, which caused me to distrust my sense of others. After the incident, I hung out by myself for a while, as much by choice as necessity. When word got out that I had informed, my former friends shunned me as if I were a murderer. It was after that, I ran away from home and became my own person.

I learned years later that a woman, a contract killer for the mob, had hit Ace and made it look like suicide after the fact.

*

Once I started telling her my story, I didn't want to stop. As long as it continued, for as long as I could keep it going, it would keep us together.

My next memory, I continued, is of a Christmas dinner at the home of my college roommate, a reclusive guy named Kevin Poole, where I developed a crush virtually at sight on his prematurely silver-haired mother, Marianna. It was a disturbing experience for me, one whose origin could be traced to a sexual flirtation I had with a nanny—I was five or six at the time—who had an equally severe personal style. Marianna was headmistress of a high-toned private girls' school in the manicured wilds of Southern Vermont and carried herself in what must have been for anyone else an off-putting military fashion, head erect, shoulders back, her voice deep and commanding. While I was falling for the improbable Marianna, Kevin's sixteen year old sister Lulu, a pouty girl who was thought to be sexy by her contemporaries, dangled herself before me like a spider web.

I tried to discourage Lulu at first, which was predictably counter-productive, but after awhile I stopped resisting and focused on the qualities she had in common with her mother, her tenacity and unbending will. I even let myself become semi-engaged to the childishly seductive girl, though I thought of it as a passing phase, a way of staying close to Marianna, who was a possessive mother.

Plans change. One day, I found myself asking Marianna for Lulu's hand, assuming the severe headmistress would say absolutely not. To my horror, I was accepted without argument. "You are the kind of serious and responsible young man," Marianna said, "I had always intended for Lulu. You couldn't be more ideal." Then she gave me a motherly kiss on the forehead to seal the bond.

The next thing I knew I was getting married, and Kevin, who was best man, was confiding that Lulu and his mother weren't the only ones in his family that felt great affection for me. It was not a confession I could readily process. High on champagne, I confided in return that I had barely controlled unrequited feelings for his mother, Marianna. Kevin took my ill-advised confession badly, professed to be shocked, even threatened to expose me. Still, the wedding came off as planned, though a perverse tension, which I may have been alone in experiencing, seemed to pervade the ceremony.

We took our honeymoon in Paris, where Marianna was attending a conference on the education of superior women. Our second night there—I was already becoming a little bored with Lulu—I took mother and daughter to dinner at Deux Maggots. We had been drinking champagne, toasting each other, toasting the marriage, toasting the conference on superior women, when Lulu, who had apparently gone beyond her capacity, passed out. Marianna and I, concerned with the bride's fragility, took her back to our hotel room, Lulu's and mine, and put her to bed.

Alone with Marianna, I was in a benumbed state, afraid that I would misbehave. We were in the sitting room of the bridal suite—our mutual charge asleep in the adjoining room— when abruptly Marianna asked me why I had married Lulu since it was plain that I didn't love her. I protested my good faith, pretended to be offended by her charge. "You are a deceiver," Marianna said, producing a gun from her purse, pointing it at my heart. As we faced each other, we were both breathing heavily as if we had walked up several flights of stairs.

I made a sudden move to take the gun away from her, which she seemed prepared for, and we struggled for several minutes with neither of us achieving a clear advantage. She was even stronger than I imagined. Eventually, she relinquished the gun and fell back on the couch. When I returned the gun to her, she accepted it with a sigh of resignation. What followed happened at some level of awareness outside consciousness. The next thing I knew we were making love, our clothes still mostly in place, using the sitting room rug as our bed, while Lulu, who had been dreaming, called my name from behind the closed door of the bedroom.

The next time we were alone, Marianna was full of regrets, promising me that what had happened would never happen again, threatening to kill us both if necessary to save her daughter's marriage. Nevertheless, a routine established itself. Each night after Lulu was asleep, Marianna would come to our suite and, pointing her gun at my heart, order me to be faithful to her daughter. And each time, I would contrive to wrestle the gun away from her, one thing leading to another, which was always the same thing: out of control lovemaking followed by recriminations and regret. We went on this way, barely escaping discovery on several occasions, for almost two weeks.

I think it was when I insisted on prolonging the honeymoon that Lulu got suspicious or perhaps she noticed my hand on her mother's knee when we were all sitting together in the hotel dining room. In any event, confused and disturbed by the unimaginable thing she sensed, Lulu wrote to Kevin, obliquely confiding her bizarre suspicions. I learned this from Kevin after he arrived in Paris and confronted me about my relationship with Marianna. It was useless to deny his accusation. He had already forced a confession from his mother, whom he had witnessed slip into our suite in the early hours of the morning, gun in hand. As soon as her son confronted her, Marianna broke down and confessed our crime.

Without telling me of her plans, Marianna ran off, taking the next available flight back to the states. Shortly after her return, she took up with an overweight sleazy writer of diet books, a brutal man even more inappropriate for her than I had been. The news travelled slowly since I went off in another direction altogether, though not by choice. Not knowing what else to do, I pursued Marianna back to the states, thinking if I could explain myself (we had done so little talking), it might make things right again. As fate would have it, I came down with an undiagnosable life-threatening fever and was hospitalized in a remote area of Newfoundland for almost nine months.

While I was out of the picture—thought to be dead perhaps—Lulu and Kevin played house together in Boston, wearing the clothes I had left behind in my hasty escape, one or the other pretending to be me, taking turns, taking my name, living together like brother and sister in a Cocteau novel. Apparently, they went on this way until I recovered (my illness disappearing as mysteriously as it had arrived), and I located them after a prolonged search, living together as husband and wife. Finding them was like finding myself. At Lulu's invitation, I stayed with them for a while, playing whatever role they offered me. When they told me Marianna had remarried, the news had too much impact for me to assimilate it. Then without warning, Lulu and Kevin took off, disappeared for a few weeks, ran off again (when found), and then again, until some black hole seemed to take them in its bosom forever.

"I really should be going," Marisan said.
"One more story," I insisted.

five

After breaking up with Lulu (and Lulu's seductive mother), I stayed on in Boston, sharing a large apartment with a former college roommate of mine, Peter Price, who was an inveterate practical joker. I don't know how it started exactly, but we got into playing tricks on one another—little things for the most part, harmless clownish stuff—the stakes gradually escalating.

I was doing a series of stretching exercises, my usual morning routine, preliminary to getting dressed for a job interview, my first serious prospect for employment since coming to Boston. While I was doing sit-ups, Peter's diminutive furry dog, Beauregard, slipped behind me and a crazy thing happened. The dog's underside, which Peter had apparently treated with Krazy Glue, affixed itself to my back. I tried everything I could think of to separate us, short of peeling my skin away, but the nasty little dog held fast. I had left myself barely enough time to make the interview, so I took the only immediate solution available to me and dressed myself, borrowing one of my larger roommate's suits, over the whining dog glued to my back. When I looked in the mirror, the appearance I gave was that of a hunchback.

It was never my intention to seek sympathy for a contrived disability—I thought of myself in fact as a walking joke—but to explain to a potential employer that a dog had accidentally got glued to my back seemed an even more disastrous route. I didn't discover this until later on, but the firm interviewing me, World Wide Distributors, had recently been fined by some government agency for not having a handicapped person in their employ. So when I showed up for my appointment with my wiggling hunch (that occasionally growled), the man in charge, Mr. Harker, seemed inexplicably pleased to meet me. He pumped my hand a number of times and said I was exactly the kind of intelligent young man they were looking for. Although I had minimal prior experience and made a fool of myself at the interview—I had to pretend the yelps of the dog were coming from my stomach and not my back—Mr. Harker offered me the job as a public relations spokesman on the spot.

My getting the job on unwittingly false pretences created further problems for me. I had to continue to wear the dog on my back or risk losing a well-paying job I was exceedingly good at. A second problem surfaced on my first day at work. Harker's charming assistant, Marie, who was also his daughter, had, it turned out, an erotic fascination with the disabled and sat on my desk almost half the day chatting me up. When she asked me for a date, I refused her, suggesting in the subtlest possible way that I took displays of pity as a form of insult. Marie persisted, would not accept my refusal. "Despite your low opinion of yourself, Max," she said, "I find you a terribly attractive man."

Each night, I took Beauregard off before going to bed, then glued him on again in the morning. It was not always easy to put him back in exactly the same spot, which meant that some days my hunch looked different from other days, which caused some raised eyebrows at work.

My first date with Marie, particularly because I couldn't dissuade her from touching my hump, became a comedy of misadventures. At one point, I noticed in the restaurant mirror that Beauregard's bushy tail was hanging out from the slit in Peter's jacket. I had to get to a bathroom to rearrange the tail before anyone else noticed. The odder my behavior, the more charmed Marie seemed to be with me. What I suspected, which made our growing intimacy difficult for me to accept, was that Marie loved me only for my hunch.

On our second date, she invited me to bed, and I told her, which was partially true, that I had had an unhappy love affair a few years back I hadn't quite gotten over.

"If you fall off a horse," she said, "the best thing to do is climb on another one."

"You'll have to give me a little more time," I said.

The deception became harder and harder to sustain—the moral difficulties almost as burdensome as the physical. I didn't like lying to people I liked. When Harker called me into his office and, after praising my performance in glowing terms, offered me a raise—this was after only four weeks in his employ—only an intuitive sense of self-preservation kept me from confessing everything then and there. I wanted nothing more than to get the dog off my back and end my deception.

So I invited Marie to my place for dinner, announcing in advance that I had something I wanted to get off my chest—an inadvertent confusion of anatomy—planning to tell her the whole story when I judged the time to be right. The prankish Peter, who was supposed to be out of the house on a date, had instead hid himself in my bedroom closet for reasons I can only speculate on. Even for Peter, who tended to have no sense of the appropriate, this was a new low. My mistake was not to confess my unwitting deception at Marie's arrival. Instead we drank martinis together, and I lost all sense of restraint, taking her to bed with no thought of the consequences. The moment after Marie told me that she loved me, she put her hand on what she thought was my hunch, and Beauregard bit her finger. That ended the deception once and for all. Marie slapped my face with her unbloodied hand and walked out, vowing to get me fired, vowing never to talk to me again. That was when Peter, unable to contain his amusement at my expense, came out of the closet. When he saw how miserable I was, he stopped laughing and said he would go after Marie and explain that what happened was not my fault. I didn't know whether to trust him—our game had long since gotten out of hand—particularly so when I noticed from the window that he was wearing an eye patch when he hit the street.

The next day I appeared at work without my hunch with, I suppose, predictable results. Marie's father called me into his office and, more in sorrow than anger, told me to leave his corporation and never come back. "You are not the son I never had I thought you were," he said.

Marie was even more unforgiving than her father. The attempts I made at reestablishing contact—phone calls, flowers, appearances at her door—were met with rebuff. Then I discovered that Peter, pretending to be blind in one eye, had established himself as her new boyfriend. That was the worst practical joke of all.

I devised a plan to get back at him. Though he was taller, really bigger in every way, I provoked a fight at a landing on the stairwell in our building and as the result of one of his punches, I fell down a flight of stairs and suffered what appeared to be a crippling injury.

I was in the hospital, in traction, when an abjectly apologetic Peter, carrying flowers, came to visit. "How bad is it, Max?" he asked. I said that if I was lucky I might be able to walk again in two years with the help of a cane. Peter, who was hunched over in his chair with his head in his hands, said, "What do you want me to do? I'll do whatever you say."

I asked him if he would put it in writing, and he said he would.

"I don't want to ever see you again," I said. "I want you to leave Boston and promise never to return."

He hesitated only a moment before agreeing to my terms. He seemed relieved by the mildness of my punishment and held out his hand, which I pretended to be too enfeebled to take.

Shortly after Peter's departure, his notarized oath of self-banishment under my pillow, Marie came in, also bearing flowers. She said that she forgave me, that she understood that people often behaved unlike themselves in periods of desperation.

When I told her in detail about the nature of my injuries, the ardor I had seen at our first meeting returned to her eyes. Did I mind, she asked in a child's importuning voice, if she got under the covers with me. I acquiesced by blinking my eyes, my neck brace preventing a nod. "If I'm hurting you," she said, "just tell me." I took my medicine, as it were, with barely a whine of complaint.

I waited an hour after Marie had gone, which, given my mood, took uncharacteristic patience, then I carefully disconnected myself from the various pulleys that held me in mummified suspension, removed my neck brace and leg cast and, while watching myself in the wall mirror, I rock-and-rolled around the room to the music of petty satisfaction. At some point, in fitting comeuppance, I tripped over a discarded bed pan and fell headlong into a wall, catching my reflection like a TV image—a cartoon figure falling on its head—as I lost consciousness, slipping from one dream to another.

six

That wasn't the last of Peter Price. A few years later, tired of working for others, I opened my own consulting firm in New York City, which did virtually anything that paid the rent, including detective work which was called private investigation. My first client was a haggard young man of about my own age, which was twenty-eight, who came to see me with the most unlikely request. The familiar young man was my banished buddy, Peter, and we forgave each other for our mutual deceptions.

Not knowing exactly what was at stake, I accompanied him to a luxury eastside apartment building and helped him talk his way into a penthouse apartment belonging to some countess who was apparently not at home on our arrival. Peter had warned me that I would see things there that my rational nature would find difficult to comprehend, but I discounted his remarks as the product of a skewed imagination. We walked on figurative tip-toes through a succession of elegant, virtually empty, seemingly unoccupied rooms, talking in whispers or not at all. In a walk-in closet adjoining a bedroom which had no bed, we discovered an Art Deco coffin, which was apparently what Peter meant for me to see, lying in a bed of designer dirt. To say I had never seen anything like it before would be only to insist on the obvious.

"So?" I asked, still skeptical, awaiting, not a little anxiously, for the punchline of the joke. He had me hold his attaché case while he snapped it open and removed a wooden stake with a pointed tip and a large wooden hammer. Uh oh, I said to myself. Peter paced the closet nervously, blotting his hands on the side of his pants.

Eventually, he approached the coffin with renewed purpose. "Max, you're here to be my witness," he said. "I want you to see what she is before I do what I came to do." Then he threw open the coffin, averting his eyes, stake and hammer under his left arm, thin wisps of white smoke, a ghostly essence, wafting from the dusty box. In the coffin was a beautiful pallid woman, dressed in a stylish black gown, gold pin of a bat over her left breast, in an unbreathing sleep. Peter held the stake above the woman's heart in his left hand, the hammer in his right, for a prolonged time, trapped in indecision. I could only imagine what was going through his mind. "Wait for me downstairs," he said. "It will be easier without you here."

I hung around outside the building for another two hours, day softening into twilight, waiting for Peter's return. When I glanced up at the apartment, I saw a woman's face—the woman in the coffin's face—framed in the window.

Was I daydreaming? It was as if time had passed without my being aware of it. I had about decided to move on when I felt a silken hand on my shoulder. It was the woman in the coffin, standing next to me in front of her building. "I haf two Dress Circle tickets for ze opera tonight," she said in a melodic, comic-opera Eastern European accent. "Vill you join me in my box?" I nodded my consent, virtually speechless.

I learned her name, which was Countess Maria Moussakka, at a cafe supper after the opera. "Am I too old for you?" she asked. "On my next birthday, I vill be two hundred and twenty-five years old."

"I have always liked older women," I said somewhat foolishly, mostly to be polite, and then I told her about my obsession with my former mother-in-law, Marianna.

When I took her home, the countess invited me in for a drink, which I declined out of an instinct for self-preservation. She was very beautiful and I was already half in love with her.

Maria made no further appeal, went inside her building as if walking on air, her red-lined black cape trailing behind her.

I walked through the park to my westside apartment, whistling to myself. It was a misty night and wisps of white smoke seemed to follow in my wake.

I was in my bedroom getting out of my clothes when I heard an unaccountable tapping noise at the window. When I opened it, a ghostly white vapor seemed to filter into the room. None of this seemed surprising. In my hot shower—I like the water almost unbearably hot—the steam seemed to merge indistinguishably with the spectral smoke. The next thing I knew, the countess Maria Moussakka was in the shower with me, wearing her elegant black dress with its odd red hood, her hand on my shoulder. We whirled around and around in the steaming shower, then collapsed, seemingly melted to our knees, the shower curtain falling, rung by rung, on top of us. Spurts of blood flashed against the shower wall like spray gun graffiti.

I woke the next morning in my own bed at first light. The shards of a dream haunted me, replaying itself in memory over and over like a catchy jingle. What was real and what was dream? I checked out the bathroom—the shower curtain was in place, not sprawled in the tub as I seemed to remember from my dreamlike adventure the previous night. When I caught my reflection in the mirror, it seemed faded, though perhaps it was from the steam in the room, this smoky, near-transparent image of myself. Full of freaky, inexplicable energy, I called the office to tell my secretary that I wouldn't be in. I was feeling not quite myself.

I was lying in bed, dozing, when Peter, looking like hell, appeared like an apparition on the other side of the room. He stood in front of my mirror to show me he had no reflection, which, he said, was the touchstone of his condition. "How do you do that trick?" I asked him, denying to myself what some part of me knew to be real. "Whatever you do, Max," he said, "don't let the countess get her fangs into you." A moment later, he seemed to vanish into smoke, and I let myself believe that my friend's transitory appearance was just another weird dream.

When I felt strong enough to get dressed, I went to visit Maria at her apartment—my obsessive idea was that Peter was trying to keep her to himself—and I found the place abandoned, the coffin not in its closet. I questioned the doorman, and he said that no one had been living in the penthouse apartment for the past six months. They had to call the police to get me to leave.

When I went into work the next day, I found an agent of the FBI (Supernatural Phenomenon Division) waiting for me at my desk. The agent, Veronika Kay, who was improbably beautiful in her own right, was one of those people who seemed to sleep in her clothes as a form of disguise. She questioned me about Maria. "Even if I knew what I don't," I said, "even if I liked you and I do, I would tell you nothing."

Veronika was not easily put off. She had been following Maria's trail for two years now, she said in her matter of fact way, and wherever the countess went—Ms. Vampire (as she was called) tended to move between New York and Paris—bizarre stuff followed. Veronika gave me her card, advising me to call as soon as Ms. Vampire reestablished contact, which was bound to happen. "Vampires, the best of them, are self-serving and heartless," she came back through the half-opened door to tell me. "You can't believe anything they say because their agenda is death." When she was gone, I discovered that she had left me a clove of garlic as a gift. Her concern amused me. I was too far gone to recognize the very real danger I was in.

Veronika's prediction was unassailable. The next evening, Maria suddenly appeared to me in front of a lamppost, seemed to transform out of smoky threads of light, looking chic and sexy in one of her new Paris gowns. She had fled to Paris, she said, to escape whatever was happening between us, but she missed me so much, she felt compelled to come back with only half her shopping completed. We embraced like ordinary lovers. I took her dancing, which she hadn't done in public, she said, for almost a hundred years.

It was past four AM when I brought her home, Maria's apartment, except for the crimson velvet drapes she had brought back from Paris, almost exactly as it had been. "Tonight," I said to her, "we're going to be just another mostly human couple."

"Ve can only be what ve are," she said. "If I fall in love, I am in danger of losing everything. It is best, my darling, you join me in my world. I vill make glorious night your everlasting morning." She put her arms around me, whirling me around and around in a feverish dance.

I dissembled, whispered in her ear that I wanted to make love to her in the human way, leaving open the possibility of reconsidering her offer.

"At my age, I do not require birth control," she said in a girlish voice, pulling me down with her to her ancestral rug.

I dawdled over the preliminaries, aware that we were no more than a half hour away from the first light of morning. "Hurry," she whispered, but I continued to move in slow motion. We had just begun to make love when the morning made itself felt, sunlight drifting through the drapes. "What haf you done to me?" she cried, the back of her hand shielding her face from the sun. I disentangled in no particular hurry, climbed to my feet.

Maria seemed to be holding herself together, sweat coming from her eyes, or was it tears? She aged fifty years in a moment like the character played by Margo in *Lost Horizons*. "Haf pity," she pleaded. "Carry me to my resting place."

I lifted her up—she seemed weightless now—and carried her through the sunlit apartment in search of her ancestral coffin. With her waning strength, she put her mouth to my throat and bit me gently, drawing blood. I fell to the floor, taking her with me. "Why?" I asked.

"'S my nature," she said ruefully in a voice so weak I might have dreamt it, disintegrating by degrees before my eyes, turning at last into a pile of dust, which seemed to spell out a word, though in no language I knew.

I was sitting in the apartment's one comfortable chair, lost in wonder and regret, wondering what other choices there might have been, when Veronika Kay rushed in, surveying the debris, assimilating the room's recent inexplicable history in a glance.

"Thank God, you're all right," she said, holding out her hand to me. "I was afraid I wouldn't get here in time." When I was on my feet again, we hugged like old friends, a celebration of survival, swinging each other around in an awkward dance, the passing image in the hall mirror of solid, fleshy, joyful Veronika spinning about to unheard music, her arms encompassing the bare outline of a figure, a fading shadow, my ghost.

Exhaustion seemed to overtake us both at the same time, and we were nodding off periodically while struggling to retain the world. It seemed cruel to go on. I suggested that we get some sleep—a few hours at least—and pick up my story in the morning.

seven

Marisan woke the next morning in a receptive mood. "You're still here," she said and kissed me. "I want to hear what comes next."

For a moment I couldn't remember where I left off.

"You were dancing with Veronika Kay," Marisan reminded me, "and you noticed that your reflection in the mirror was ghostly, almost invisible."

My reflection. My reflection returned in sharp focus about the time my memory of Maria Moussakka died. The period of mourning and recuperation had lasted approximately six months and I found myself back in school, studying Applied Biology, for which I showed unexpected flair. I was interested, I confess, less in benefiting mankind at this time in my life than in developing knowledge for its own sake. "You ought to have been here when Dr. Y was around," said one of my teachers in response to a paper I had written. "He was after the same mystifying quarry as you."

The next time I heard of Dr. Y was at a Popular Science symposium sponsored by The Meaning of Life Society at the university. The group of famous scientists on stage got into a heated discussion as to who was the greatest scientist of all time pursuing a career of no redeeming social value.

Three out of the five panelists cited Dr. Y as the man most deserving of that distinction. One of the panelists, who said he had studied with the visionary doctor at Leeds, where he had developed a frog capable of singing "God Save the Queen," called him "the most brilliant misguided scientist I ever had the misfortune to know."

Intrigued, I went to the library and read everything I could find by Dr. Y, including an article published in the *Journal of Animal Semiotics* on how to speed up the evolutionary process between pre-human species and humans. The article moved me like a poem; in reading it, I felt I had connected with my other self. So I wrote Dr. Y a fan letter—he had been living on an obscure volcanic island in the south Atlantic—telling him how much I admired his work and how it was my dream as a young scientist to study under his tutelage.

My impulsive letter to Dr. Y changed the course of my life for the next few years. Two weeks later I received a letter postmarked Primavera Island, inviting me to witness the great scientist's "little fling at creation." The opportunity to work with this man, who had become my idol, was irresistible. I gave up everything, my apartment, my schoolwork, my fiancée Veronika Kay, to make the arduous trip to Primavera.

There was no direct route to Primavera, the island beyond the bounds of recorded civilization. The trip took a full three months to make, including a prolonged stay on another island—the boat I had chartered foundered in a storm—a hundred miles to the north. El Nuevo Mundo, as it was called, had been colonized by the Spaniards in the 15th century and had been forgotten by the world. ENM was governed by descendants of the Inquisition, who continued over the centuries to keep the faith by reenacting the Redemption of Man with each new generation. I was chosen to play the redeemer, which seemed an exciting prospect until I learned that none of my predecessors in the role had survived. I escaped the island the night before the ritual was scheduled to be enacted.

When I finally reached Primavera—I travelled the remaining distance on a wooden raft using the limb of a tree as an oar—I was barely alive, running a dangerously high fever and hallucinating. A woman with the head of a sheep, who introduced herself as Dr. Y's assistant, greeted me on my arrival and led me—I have no memory of the details—to my quarters in an underground building.

On my third (or fourth) day on Primavera—it was a place without clocks, without reference to time—my fever abruptly and irrevocably gone, I was granted my first audience with Dr. Y, a spiderlike man of extraordinary height, who wore the same fez-like cap and starched white labcoat for all occasions. Satisfied that my health had sufficiently improved, Y took me on a tour of the small island, showing me the astonishing results of his attempts to evolve human life in his own image from the various creatures on the island. Everyone in the stratified world the doctor had created bore some resemblance to its creator.

I congratulated the eccentric doctor on his accomplishments and indicated that I was looking forward to taking a hand in the process. He waved off my compliments in his characteristically modest way. "Failures," he said, "all failures. I am only an imperfect god."

It was only at the highest level that Y seemed to fail—his highly evolved animals retaining traces of their original state, never becoming fully human. "What is lacking," said Y, "is the intangible soul. When I find the formula for the human soul then my fling at creation will be complete."

I worked as Y's assistant for about a year without ever being taken fully into his confidence. Gradually, in imperceptible ways, my exalted opinion of the man declined. His repeated cruelties to what he perceived to be his failures were hard to abide. "The formula is right," he would say. "It is the creature who insists on hanging on to its brutish nature." Perceived failures tended to be retrenched and used "to extend the limits of scientic knowledge." Creatures disappeared every day without explanation and without a trace. To keep my belief system from eroding altogether, I had to invent alternate scenarios to explain the unacceptable.

The only other unequivocal human on the island was the doctor's beautiful wife, Maribeau, who would come to my room those evenings the doctor worked late to talk about her loneliness. The doctor himself was always available to talk— he was a brilliant lecturer with a tendency to monomaniacal obsession—but never, alas, available to listen. He was a man, like most autocrats, who heard only his own voice.

It was Maribeau, who told me that the duck-woman, Ida, who was my chess partner and confidante, an almost human creature with webbed fingers and the embryonic bill of a duck, was scheduled for reasons that seemed pure arbitrariness to be deevolved. We were both horrified at the news. With Maribeau's help, I made contact with the brutish rebel forces who had formed an underground society on another part of the island. In the end, I led the rebels against the man I had once admired above all others. Our mission had limited goals. Our intent was not to harm the doctor if at all possible, merely restrain him from further inhuman excess. With my help, the rebels rescued the duck-woman and effected a bloodless coup.

The aggrieved partial humans submitted a list of demands to their deposed leader, whom they had once worshipped as a god, a list which included a cessation of the programatic genocide toward perceived failures and a six-day fifty-hour work week. Y, who had treated his overthrow with the same disdain he had for any irrational behavior, acceded to the demands of "his children," as he called them. "Almost humans," he said, "are deserving of almost human rights."

Everyone seemed pleased with the new accord—democracy had come to Primavera Island as the inevitable next step. I remember writing in my journal that Dr. Y was truly, as he sometimes jokingly called himself, the man who invented the world.

That night, shortly after Y had been restored to power, the rebel leaders, myself included, were seized while we slept and imprisoned in the Red Room, a dungeon-like place I had never been privileged to see before. This was the arena where the most bizarre and unnatural experiments took place. Y had planned a system of elaborate punishments for us that it amused him to see as appropriate to our crimes. He had never given the fluid that reversed the evolutionary process to a natural human before, he told me, and was eager for the sake of science to see the results. "You will be your own doctoral thesis," he told me, his eyes rampaging like cattle gone mad.

Primavera, as I mentioned earlier, was a volcanic island—a potentially imminent danger. "At any given moment," Y often announced, "all that I've created can be turned to dust." Just as the doctor was about to inject me with the retrograde fluid, the volcano chose to erupt, and the island began to tear itself apart. A sudden jolt caused the doctor's hand to slip, and the needle missed me and stabbed Y in the leg. After that, buildings collapsing, thousand year old trees being torn from the ground by their roots, we all fled for our lives. I found myself in a small boat with four of my fellow rebels, and as we moved off toward the mainland, we watched the island come apart in a series of volcanic explosions, a huge mushroom cloud hovering above the flames.

I returned to the states alone ten days later—as soon as we reached the mainland my colleagues reverted in rapid order to the animals they once had been—with only my memory to account for the experience I had just described to you. I had not seen Y escape and could only assume that the doctor had gone down with his island like the skipper of a ship. I felt as if I had lost my greater self.

And then one day—I was back at the university writing up the results of my stay on Primavera—I got a call from a woman who said she was Maribeau Y, asking if she could meet me for a drink at one of the university district cafes. I waited for her at an outdoor table, nervously sipping absinthe as if it were an intravenal fluid, not knowing what to expect from Maribeau's visit. She was a half hour late, and I was ready to give up on her and go back to my study, when I saw this beautiful dark woman at the end of the street slowly coming toward me. It was clearly Maribeau, and she was being pulled along by a large dog, who seemed unused to the constraints of a leash, the dog wearing, I noticed to my horror, the white lab coat and fezlike cap I had last seen on Dr. Y.

I fell asleep at some point, and when I awoke Marisan was gone. "Don't try to find me," her note said. "Goodbye. Goodbye. Goodbye."

eight

I took a cab to Kennedy Airport and after an extended search found Marisan at Gate 12 about to board the next TWA flight to San Francisco. When she saw me, she left the boarding line and walked away in no particular direction. I followed her as I had before, staying just close enough to keep her in view. She went from building to building, moving through the crowds, picking up my reflection in the wall mirror from time to time, never actually looking back. When she returned to Gate 12 about forty minutes later, her flight, which was also mine, had already departed. She refused to look at me, and I honored her decision by not approaching her.

An hour or so later—by then we had covered virtually the entire airport—Marisan collapsed in front of the luggage carousel connected with some obscure Belgian airline, and an ambulance was summoned before I could get to her side.

"Take me back to our hotel," she whispered to me as soon as I reached her.

I lifted her up against the protests of the airport security and random bystanders, and I carried her down the escalator and out of the airport. People tried to stop us, but I pushed my way through them and hailed a cab. I had no doubts that she was dying.

Marisan revived when we got back to the hotel room and was her old self for a while, sitting up in bed and singing, her eyes bright.

"Tell me some more of your story, Max," she said.

"Don't you think you should get some rest first?"

"The story first," she said in a playful voice. "The rest will wait."

So I continued.

Once you get into the fever of inventing things, my next story started, it's hard to go back to the dailiness of ordinary science. I had a university job as a biology prof, but I rarely got to my classes on time and often, caught up obsessively in my work, skipped them altogether. Dr. Y's example haunted me. I had a credo posted on the wall of my lab, "Science without moral restraint is the universe run amok." As I neared the completion of my project, which had to do with the deconstruction of the space/time continuum, I went for days without sleep and sustained myself almost solely on coffee and granola bars.

In a hurry to learn first hand the implications of my almost completed invention, I took the place of one of my guinea pigs in an experiment that involved what turned out to be unacceptable risk. The experiment, which was a partial success, moved me a year into the future (took a year out of my life), and I found myself no longer at the university (the destruction of my lab had cost me my job) but at sea again, as First Mate and Science Officer, on a bizarre expedition captained by the notorious impressario, Commander Bill Bucks.

The obsessive Bucks kept a journal of the ill-starred voyage. "Nothing much happened today," he wrote each day in his log. At night, Bucks was unable to sleep, made anxious by the dark, tormented by dreams of impotence that seemed to waft before his eyes like smoke. Before the publication of his journal, no one knew of his affliction, not even his assistant, the beautiful and vulnerable anthropologist, Lola Monet, who is presently my estranged wife.

The journal entries had become increasingly bleak. "Unseasonably bad weather, fog everywhere, rations low," Commander Bucks wrote in his journal. "Reduced to eating the bread of affliction. Rats leaving the ship in unprecedented numbers."

And then without warning, as if it had a mind of its own, the fog lifted to reveal the uncharted island, Amoranta, like a small black cross in the distance. That night the impressario called a meeting of the tired and ragged crew to reveal the mission of the voyage. "We've come to Amoranta Island to bring back a great star who has yet to make its presence in the firmament known," he announced. A muted eeriness pervaded the restrained shipboard celebration.

On three separate occasions, drunken crew members tried to interfere with Lola, who was the only woman aboard, and I took it as my responsibility as First Mate to keep her from harm. There was something erotic in the very atmosphere of Amoranta. Lola remarked on it to Commander Bucks, who acknowledged that there was a legend to the effect that the deeper one penetrated into the heart of the island, the more potent the erotic influence.

One of the party was bitten in the leg by a snake, and Lola, who had some training as a nurse, drew off the poison with her mouth.

The first time Lola and I were alone, screened from the others by a waterfall, I found myself kissing her. Our knees seemed to melt from the heat of our embrace. We were not ourselves here or perhaps we were more totally ourselves than we had ever acknowledged in the remote and forgotten civilized world.

Moments later, the entire expeditionary force was surrounded by a band of savage pygmies. Bucks, the only one who spoke their primitive squall, conversed with the group's leader. According to Bucks, the diminutive savages were intent on taking Lola as their white queen. A queen of opposing color had been a long-standing tradition in their country. Odd growling sounds like some monumental indigestion seemed to come from behind the high walls of the fortress and sent tremors of fear through the populace.

When Bucks reported that the pygmies would allow us to return to our ship if we handed over Lola, which he saw as our only option, I opposed his plan, which included a daring moonlight rescue the following night, and accused him of being a dissembler. "You have made yourself an enemy, sir," Bucks said to me, which turned out to be prophetic. It was Bucks' malicious influence several years later that banished me from Hollywood.

Lola put the best light on her unhappy situation, said she welcomed the challenge of her queenship, that her background and training had prepared her for a position of authority in a primitive culture almost ready to make its entrance into the civilized world.

When Bucks and his small band of adventurers went back to the ship, I slipped away and followed Lola and her pygmy captors to their exotic village.

Lola had been stripped to the waist and garlanded about the breasts and neck with chains of red flowers. As she reclined on the hammock-like throne, each of the males of the tribe paid her homage by shooting sperm in the air like a fireworks display while chanting "Dong. Dong. Dong." Lola seemed to take the homage ritual in stride as if it was part of what she felt life held in store.

It happened so unexpectedly, the giant black hand reaching over the twenty-foot wall and lifting the queen from her primitive throne, that I couldn't say under oath exactly what it was I had seen.

A giant ape held Lola in the palm of his hand—I watched them from an overhanging cliff—an impassive expression on its wizened face.

"Me Lola," she said, pointing to herself.

Prince Dong, which was the name we came to know him by, nodded in apparent understanding. Watching them through field glasses, I could tell that the creature was smitten by Lola, moved as we all had been by her unassuming courage and vulnerability, her sensual mouth and starlet eyes. The sigh that passed from the creature was almost human.

I followed Dong's enormous footsteps through the maze of the jungle, stopping from time to time to call out Lola's name, the sound echoing back. The erotic pull of the landscape was so powerful, I found myself embracing a tree in desperation. I had lost all sense of the appropriate.

When I finally reached Dong's cave—the path strewn with the broken bodies of what I assumed were former brides—I called to Lola from a jutting cliff just below the giant ape's lair. When she recognized me, Lola waved, then started running toward me. Going down the side of a cliff, she tripped on a root and fell headlong. I was holding her head in my lap when she regained consciousness.

Dong, who had been asleep, let out an ear-shattering roar

when he discovered Lola's absence. When he saw us together, his grief turned abruptly to murderous rage. Here was a creature who, unlike the rest of us, lived uncompromisingly within his own skin.

"Leave him to me," said Lola, interposing herself between us.

Dong lifted her in his hand, squeezing her just enough to let her know he was a monster of displeasure.

While I looked on from behind a rock, Lola tamed the beast, soft-talked and scolded him into docility. When Dong no longer seemed murderous, she introduced him to me. "This is my brother, Max," she said to Dong. "This is Prince Dong, lord of Amoranta Island," she said to me. "I want you two to be fast friends."

Dong probed me with a gnarled finger, knocking me back and over, laughing apishly.

I spent the next week with them in Dong's lair, the three of us living together in domestic compromise.

I had made up my mind to leave, and I asked Lola, when Dong was off on an errand, to come with me. She said she couldn't, refusing to explain herself, and we got into an argument, which led to a physical struggle, the two of us thrashing about on a mound of twigs and prehistoric moss. The fight ended in love as these things do even in the darkest backwaters of the world. The island had won us to its creed.

There was no chance to reflect on what had happened between us. In the next moment, Commander Bucks and my fellow crew members arrived on the scene, armed with huge nets and an arsenal of stun guns. It was Bucks' plan to take Dong back and make a film star of him, and he wanted us, Lola in particular, to persuade the ape to come along without a fight.

Lola refused at first, said the removal of Dong from his homeland might create a serious ecological imbalance, but Bucks was a fast and persuasive talker.

"Dong will make so much money in pictures," he said with that assurance he had of being right about everything, "any lifestyle he wants will be available to him. I don't think it's fair to deny him this opportunity, do you?"

It was clear that Bucks would take Dong away with or without her participation, so Lola made conditions. Lola said she would help the impressario bring the ape to America so long as Bucks promised that if things didn't work out with Dong's career, or if Dong was unhappy or ill, he would see to it personally that the ape be returned to his island. Bucks, who turned out in the end to be both more and less contemptible than I had been persuaded to believe, gave his word. I was witness to it.

And so we took the Lord of Amoranta—the Prince of Dongness, as Bucks had labelled him, back with us to America.

As Marisan had fallen asleep, I stopped the story here.

nine

On the return trip, as a security precaution, the great ape was kept in the hull of the ship in chains. When I protested Dong's inhumane treatment, I was told by Commander Bucks, strutting about on deck with his swagger stick, that unless Dong was sufficiently broken he would never make it in the civilized world. We could hear the lovesick ape moaning from time to time in an almost human voice. During my visits to him in the hull, I was saddened by the changes civilization had wrought on the displaced creature. He had taken to smoking a pipe, a gift from Lola whose picture the ape kept on the wall of his quarters. I regretted then, and would continue to regret, my complicity in his removal from Amoranta Island.

Lola and I were rarely alone and barely talked to one another on the voyage home—our only contact the occasional wan smile across a crowded deck. It was understood that what had happened between us on the island would not be repeated.

True to his promise, the impressario starred Dong in a motion picture, treating in a semi-fictional way the giant ape's early life on prehistoric Amoranta Island. The audience at the premiere, which I reluctantly attended, gave the film a prolonged standing ovation. Prince Dong was launched on a brilliant if ultimately abortive career.

Commander Bucks, who had a flair for excess, arranged for the construction of a gigantic mansion for Dong overlooking the Pacific Ocean, the interior decor simulating the landscape of Amoranta Island. Although apparently puzzled by the unfamiliar similarities, Dong accepted the gift with what we thought of as his usual apish grace. Lola stayed with him in the massive estate as friend and advisor, and there was gossip in the prints of a secret marriage.

I stayed out on the coast for a while writing screenplays and doing some acting, but mostly I was there to look after Lola, a role that had stuck to me like tar since shipboard days. Lola was in trouble, and she was too close to the cause of her grief to recognize the problem. Dong was not the same ape she had known on the island. Success had gone to his head, and he had become increasingly careless of Lola's feelings. Other women, starlets and would-be starlets, the famous and the infamous, came to his exotic Malibu residence at all hours of the night to pay sexual homage to the celebrated beast.

It went on this way for a while. The creature had gone from extreme innocence to black-hearted depravity without the normal sidesteps and byways civilization usually supplies. Dong was prey to every fashionable vice. At one point, he had a sandbox built in his bedroom and had it filled with the whitest cocaine money could buy.

Whenever Lola threatened to leave Dong, the sly ape turned maudlin, groaning and weeping in a heartbreaking way, promising her that if she stayed with him (and only then), he would mend his ways. Dong would reform for a couple of days, just long enough to get Lola off his case, and then lapse again into the decadent mode that characterized his Hollywood tenure. He was downing gallon bottles of vodka as if they were shot glasses.

His depravity carried over into his work. He terrorized directors and co-stars with impunity, knowing he wouldn't be dropped from a project because there was no one quite like him to take his place. When the wunderkind director of his most recent film, *Dong 3: The Great Ape of the Western World*, walked off the set rather than be humiliated by his erratic star, the aroused beast destroyed over a million dollars worth of simulated jungle. The studio head, a former mob boss, was ready to cut his losses by releasing Dong from his contract.

Lola had to plead with the studio head to take Dong back. Only if Lola agreed to appear in the picture with him would he work with the ape again, he said. Committed to seeing Dong through his ordeal, Lola put aside the anthropological study she was working on to become the ape's co-star.

Lola was able to keep Dong in line for the duration of the film and *Dong 3* was completed almost on schedule. Just as it seemed that Dong had gotten his life in working order, the ape learned that Lola had received the lion's share of the press—Lola becoming a celebrity in her own right—and he hit the sauce again in a major way. Dong's epic bender made Ray Milland's in *The Lost Weekend* seem a marvel of restraint.

One day, working on his first B film—something called *Going Ape* in which I also had a part—Dong collapsed on the set and had to be taken home and put to bed. The studio sent a doctor over to examine him and I could tell from the doctor's face that there was something gravely wrong with the troubled ape. "The important thing," the doctor told Lola, "is that he want to live." It was a line he once delivered in a movie in which he played a doctor on just such an errand.

I was at the house at the time, consoling Lola, whose affection for the ape was a lot more sincere than the Hollywood community was willing to believe. Having kept her unhappiness bottled up for a long time, she let it all spill out, crying on my shoulder, one thing leading to another. "Isn't it terrible?" she said. "Max, he had the world in his hand and he threw it away."

For months, I had been imploring her to leave Dong, but I didn't want what happened next. Unhappiness is like a flame run amok. When we made love—it seemed inevitable and irresistible—it was as though we were dancing at the center of that flame.

Some intuition woke Dong from his stupor and he staggered to his feet. From the way he responded, he must have overheard some of the things Lola said to me about him.

"Max," Lola said in the aftermath of our lovemaking, "I can't leave him, not while he's ill, I can't. I'll nurse him back to health and, when he's on his feet again, tell him about us."

That was all Dong needed to hear. He mouthed Lola's name—he had become more human as the rest of us became less—and he stumbled wearily from the house onto the terraced beach that led to the ocean.

In four steps he was at the water's edge. And then, hesitating a moment—perhaps only to locate his destination—he entered the water.

When Lola discovered that the ape had gone, she pushed me away and rushed after him, following his huge tracks. "Come back, Dong," Lola called, panic driving her to the water's edge. "Dong, come back." He was already beyond the range of her voice.

Word traveled fast in Hollywood when a valuable property tried to break contract. Suddenly a helicopter appeared from nowhere and circled over Dong's head, a stream of machine gun fire kicking up the water in front of him. Dong swatted at the helicopter halfheartedly, unimpressed by its insect pretenses.

It was all out of our hands now. I stood next to Lola, holding her back, watching Dong who was almost imperceptible in the distance, a shadowy head above the waves. A second helicopter arrived and then a third.

A chauffeured white limo drove onto the beach. Commander Bucks and the head of the studio that owned Dong's contract emerged from the car.

"Where the fuck does he think he's going?" said the studio head. "The pig-headed ape is still under contract."

"He's going home," said Bucks. "I can feel his loss as if some piece of me has gone with him. That ape brought the gift of love to this town."

"Whatever he brought, it was probably something we were better off without," said the studio head, who was spitting mad.

The sun was setting. Eventually, the limousine drove off. Lola pushed my hand away when I tried to move her. "I'll see you at the house," she said. There were tears in her eyes.

I walked up the terraced beach to Dong's palatial estate, then turned back to keep vigil. It was almost completely dark now, the moon a knife slash in the gray flesh of the sky. The onlookers were leaving now in droves, some lamenting the loss of Dong, others looking for a new thrill, anything to deflect the boredom and emptiness of their lives.

Lola was alone on the beach staring out into the impenetrable ocean. And where was Dong? How far had his walk across the ocean taken him?

The night was black like an immense ape. Someone or something I couldn't see—a shadow, an imagined lover, a dream—was there with Lola. "Dong," I heard her cry. "My lovely Dong."

I could swear I saw them thrash about in the wet sand, barely illuminated by the slash of moonlight. At the highest point of the neighbor's dune, I saw a cameraman, one of the up-and-coming talents, filming the event with floodlights.

One moment Dong was there with Lola, and the next moment he was gone.

Two months after that Lola and I were married, and three months after that we were just another former couple in a city that despised the past.

"How sad," Marisan said and cried for me.

ten

During the years of Dong's reign in Hollywood, I had made some inroads myself as a screenwriter and actor, inconsequential stuff, stuff of modest ambition. In the beginning it was just something to do, but as I got into it, I gradually realized that I had begun a new and fascinating career.

About two months after Dong's fateful disappearance, Lola and I got married, going on impulse at three in the morning to the local Justice of the Peace. It was an attempt, half-hearted perhaps, to bring some stability to our fragmented lives. We lived together for a while longer, but with Dong out of the picture, there seemed no purpose to our relationship. When I went on location in England to direct one of my screenplays, *The Return of the Screw*, which was a sequel to a classic ghost story, Lola asked for a trial separation.

Bill Bucks was the producer on the film, and some of the old enmity from the Dong days remained in the air between us. He put me on notice that if the principal shooting on location at a castle in the north of England was not completed in thirty-three days, he would replace me. He also wanted to see dailies, and if the film diverged in any way from the approved script, he was prepared, he said, to pull me off the set at a moment's notice. In short, I was directing my first feature with an enemy at my throat and a gun to my head.

Each day I altered the script just enough to keep me interested and to keep the actors on their toes.

Originally, the movie started with a voice-over on a ghostly black screen, intoning, "No one knows what awaits us in the land to which we travel when our time on earth is spent, but there are some who have the power, often unknown to themselves, to see glimpses of what to the rest of us remains unseen." A woman in her forties, with a troubled past, is beginning her tour of duty as governess at the somber though splendid estate, Unmannerly, in the craggy north country of England. Her employer, Syracuse, a dark brooding figure of unpredictable moods and large family fortune, introduces her to her two preteen charges, Henry and Louise, whose mother, Sophia, has recently leaped to her death under mysterious circumstances from the Dashit Cliffs.

In the original script, the whole movie was to be seen through the hysterical governess's eyes, which meant the ghosts, which we would also see, might be a figment of an overheated imagination. Then in one of my rewrites, I had Syracuse see the ghosts, which meant the ghosts had to have some kind of objective ghostly existence.

Anyway, I had the governess keeping a diary in which she took Syracuse's civility—he had spoken to her only once— for romantic interest. But in later versions Syracuse grew to admire the governess's basic decency and loyalty, which meant we had to shorten her skirts and show a little leg. During the first two weeks of shooting, her age fell from 45 to 33, and it was clear to anyone who had eyes that the governess's mousy, repressed exterior masked a semi-beautiful smoldering sexual creature.

The housekeeper, Frau Von Bitter, reputed to have been a mistress of Hitler in his pre-political days, tyrannizes the governess while pretending to be her friend and advisor. The distracted Syracuse lets Von Bitter run Unmannerly with a free tyrannical hand, devoting himself almost exclusively to the capricious dictates of his moods.

Syracuse gives the governess her instructions concerning the children, which are undermined by Von Bitter's calculated subversion. What she is there to do, says Syracuse, is give the children a sense of English values, educate them in the classics, and keep them out of his way when he is in the thrall of one of his glowering moods. Also, says Syracuse, they are on no account to go near the Dashit Cliffs, occasion of considerable family tragedy.

The children, with whom she forms a strong attachment on sight, tend to be docile and passive in all respects except two. They lie shamelessly and they tend to wander off to the Dashit Cliffs, despite her grave warning against such folly, at any and every opportunity. Something is pulling them toward the cliffs, and she (I had deliberately not given her a name, though Bucks had pressed me to call her Jane) becomes obsessed with protecting them from their own self-destructive impulses.

When she follows her charges to the cliffs, she observes them talking to the spectral figure of a woman who seems to be tempting them to step over the edge. Jane rushes to their side and, though terrified of heights, pulls them back to safety. The spectral figure vanishes.

Jane reports the episode to Syracuse, who seems unsurprised by her news and asks her to describe the ghost. "I never said it was a ghost," says Jane. The woman she saw, she says, resembles the portrait on the wall of his wife, Sophia. (Frau Von Bitter spies on this conversation from behind a curtain, a sly malicious look on her face.) In one version, Syracuse dismisses her report as hysterical delusion. In another, he makes Jane promise to take him with her when she follows the mischievous children the following night.

Frau Von Bitter confronts her and threatens to have her fired for disturbing the master with her ravings. "It is loony to believe in ghosts," says Von Bitter, and lets her know that she is aware of Jane's recent sojourn in a mental institution. Jane returns to her room and packs her bags. At some point, she discovers a mean-looking snake in her bed, which she pretends doesn't exist, lying down next to it with her arms frozen at her sides.

Waking from a suffocating dream, she rushes to the window and discovers Louise (who has aged from 11 to 16 over three drafts) following the apparent ghost of Sophia in the direction of the Dashit Cliffs, their way lit by a strangely luminous moon. "I can't leave without solving the mystery," she writes in her diary. "I am all but certain that something at Unmannerly is trying to do mischief to these children I love with all my heart."

As she follows Louise, who is being lured to the cliffs, she becomes aware that something not altogether human is following her. It is another spectral form, and it is pointing to its mouth as if it wants to confide something of importance. Jane indicates that she is receptive to its message. When it speaks, it is as if the wind is talking to her. "Save her," the wind seems to say. "Save her." "I promise," she says, "but tell me who you are." Lights flash, but no answer is given, and the ghost disappears. Ghosts, one learns, whatever else their powers, are unable to speak their names in the presence of the living. The first ghost floats seductively at the edge of a precipice, beckoning Louise toward her. "Louise, stop where you are this instant," Jane says in her governess voice. "That woman is not your mother."

Louise is balanced awkwardly at the edge of the cliff, her head half-turned toward Jane, the ghost flickering ahead of her, holding out its arms with false promise. The second spectral figure appears and interposes its vaporous form between Louise and ghost one. At that point we recognize that the two ghosts are virtually identical. Jane looks on in astonishment, unable to move.

Trying to retreat from the precipice, Louise loses her balance and falls forward into the void. In a desperate lunge, Jane grabs Louise out of the air and deposits her charge on firm ground. The danger registering after it has passed, Jane collapses in a hysterical faint. Louise revives the governess with a kiss on the cheek. The second ghost throws itself against the first, and the two fall, as they had once in life, to the jagged rocks below.

Syracuse, who has arrived on the scene, relieved to see Louise and Jane unharmed, tells his daughter and her governess the strange story of the two ghosts. "I've kept this secret to myself for too long a time," he says.

Twenty odd years ago, he fell in love and married a beautiful sweet-natured orphan named Sophia, with whom he lived in marital bliss for nine years when—it was about the time Frau Von Bitter arrived—she seemed to become another person. What actually happened was that the real Sophia was murdered at that time by her jealous twin, thrown off Dashit Cliffs to the jagged rocks below, the surviving sister then posing as the woman she murdered. At that point, Syracuse had no knowledge that Sophia had ever had a twin sister.

For years, Syracuse sensed that something was wrong, that his innocent wife had changed into a cynical shrew, but until he read the second Sophia's journal, he had no way of verifying his suspicion. Once he knew for sure—there were other telltale signs to give away the imposture (one had a mole in a certain place and the other didn't)—Syracuse and the imposter-wife had a terrible fight, which ended with Syracuse accidentally killing her. He then took her dead body and threw it off the cliffs at the same spot the real Sophia had fallen. (In an earlier version, he made her show him where she had killed Sophia, and then killed her in the same way at the same place.) Frau Von Bitter, who had loved the evil Sophia and had witnessed both murders, has warned Syracuse that she would expose him unless he gave her free reign at Unmannerly. Syracuse tells this story to Jane and Louise while riding back to Unmannerly by horse-drawn carriage.

When they return to Unmannerly, they discover much has changed in their absence. Frau Von Bitter has attempted to kill Henry (in one version she actually does) and has burnt the estate to the ground. When Jane is alone with her thoughts, the evil Von Bitter (who is really a man in disguise—this a late hour choice) attacks her with a large kitchen knife. Syracuse arrives in time to save her, killing Frau Von Bitter while being fatally wounded himself. In his dying breath, Syracuse tells Jane that he wants her to marry him, and the ceremony is held on the spot, Syracuse dying moments after the vows have been taken.

Soundings that Bucks took indicated that an audience wanted Syracuse to survive his fatal wounds and live happily ever after with Jane as his wife. I reshot the ending under protest, keeping a pirated copy of the original cut. The film ends in the official version with Jane and Syracuse walking like shadows through the ashes of Unmannerly. The only touch of mine that survives is a ghostly laugh on the soundtrack as the screen fades to black.

When I protested Bucks' treatment of my film, we got into a heated argument, and I said some things I would live to regret. "You'll never work in this industry again while I have the power to keep you out," he told me. As always, he was as good as his word. After eighteen months of struggling to find an open door, I grudgingly accepted Bucks' verdict and left

Hollywood without a backward glance. My plan was to go north for a few years, go back to school and try my hand at a new discipline—either psychiatry or high finance (I had learned by then that money equaled power)—and then return triumphantly and reestablish my career under a new name. I had more movies in me than the unlamented "Return of the Screw," which was never released in theaters and was bartered to Video under the title, *Sophia's Ghost* with the directorial credit excised from the box.

I was on a return flight from a business deal in Paris (with stopovers in Brussels, Milan and Beirut) when chance put me in the seat next to you, and, as a result of our meeting, as a result of our falling in love, my plans for the future abruptly changed. We followed each other through the city and then I lost you—we lost each other—and the pain of that loss made me want to stay with you for as long as I could, so we took a room at the Hotel Paradise, and we told each other our stories.

"I'm dying for an egg salad sandwich, Max," Marisan said. "Do you think you could find one for me at this hour of the night? Whole wheat would be the bread of preference."

I was afraid to leave her, afraid that one way or another she'd be gone on my return. Even though I knew it was a mistake to let her out of my sight, I couldn't gracefully refuse her request.

And yet what happened next was wholly unforeseen. I was in an all night Korean grocery ordering food for us when two men in ski masks came in and held up the store. The owner of the grocery took a gun from under the counter and shot one of them. The other panicked and fired randomly, hitting me in the temple with one of his shots. I woke three days later in a hospital with most of my memory gone. The only thing I had to hold on to was the nagging feeling that someone somewhere was waiting for me to return.

Without a memory, I was like a child. The days passed uneventfully, and I still didn't know my name. The few memories that flashed in my brain were like coded images on a screen. The little I remembered of my life seemed to have only marginal relation to my inner core. An airline commercial on a television screen filled me with a sense of undefined urgency. I had a San Francisco driver's license in my wallet, which provided me with my only clue.

*

I discharged myself from the hospital that night, though my motor abilities were still extremely limited and I tended to lose my balance after four or five steps. It took me an hour to accomplish what in ordinary circumstances might take at most ten minutes. I took a cab to the airport and, following the same hunch that had impelled me to leave the hospital, got on a flight to San Francisco, where the answer to whatever it was I had lost seemed to be awaiting me.

part 2

eleven

Unable to remember the point of my former job or even the job itself, unable to remember who was waiting for me and where, I set up shop in San Francisco as a private investigator, hoping along the way I would solve the case of the missing person in myself.

I had taken the name Max Aant as a way of getting a listing in the phone book ahead of my competitors, which for the first several weeks brought in only the most tawdry business off the street. I may have lost much of my past, including a sense of self, but I still had some scruples left, which meant I had to reject most of my opportunities. And then late one afternoon, I got a call from a Dr. Linus Poole, a New Wave Mill Valley therapist specializing in inexplicable neuroses, summoning me to his office for a consultation.

Poole was an intense, well-spoken man in his fifties with a Mephistopholean beard. His office represented the latest in Northern California hi-tech. "I've heard good things about you," was the first thing he said after we shook hands. I couldn't imagine from whom, though I accepted the compliment in good grace. He was worried about his wife, Veronika, who had just returned from a field trip to Haiti, where she had been researching a definitive study on meta-death phenomena, in an "odd benumbed state." Since her return home, she tended to rise during the night without waking and wander mysteriously from the house. My job was to follow Mrs. Poole on her wanderings and give Dr. Poole a moment-to-moment report of her activities.

Was this just another divorce case in exotic disguise? I wondered.

That very night I trailed Veronika, who indeed seemed to be walking in her sleep, to an open field adjoining a graveyard. A unusual ceremony was going on in the field, people wearing grotesque masks and beating on exotic drums, Veronika at the center of the crowd's attention. What happened next was so extraordinary that even my own witness of it seemed insufficient proof that it was real. Nor was it the kind of thing I would have accepted as fact from even the most unimpeachable of authorities. As the drums reached an orgiastic beat, Veronika rose from the ground and seemed to fly over the field. I tried to run after the flying figure without giving myself away and in the process I lost her, if indeed the large wingless bird overhead was really Veronika Poole. Haunted by hallucinations since my head wound, I had no reason to trust the testimony of my sight. A snake with a human head appeared at the entrance to the graveyard and I fled the chimera in despair at my own weakness.

I reported what I thought I had seen to Dr. Poole and was praised for my diligence and sent out a second time on the same errand.

This time I followed Veronika to a woods beyond the graveyard and found myself observing what I assumed was a Voodoo ceremony. Veronika didn't fly this time, but was at the center of a kind of orgiastic dance, whirling faster and faster, impelled by the frantic rhythm of the drums. Without warning, she collapsed to the ground in a faint. She seemed dead or close to it when I reached her, but I lifted her up nevertheless (my movements mechanical enough to be taken for one of the somnambulistic celebrants), and I carried her to my car while grotesque specters, their arms outstretched, pursued us in retarded motion.

Veronika didn't want to go home—she had a moment of lucidity in the car—so I took her to my place for want of another choice and put her down in my unmade bed. While I was straightening up, I noticed two dead ants in my bathtub and a warning on the medicine cabinet mirror, written in blood,

"Kiss off, Aant." What happened next was stranger still. I called Dr. Poole to make my report and he told me that his wife had returned to him unharmed. "Are you sure of that?" I asked him, checking the bedroom to confirm that Veronika was indeed where I had left her.

"Some of my patients have been upset by the adverse publicity your investigation has attracted," he said. "My clinic depends on favorable public perception for its survival. So as much as I personally would like to have you around—your reports are as entertaining as any I've seen—necessity dictates the termination of your services."

"Doctor," I said, aware that Veronika was signalling to me not to give her away, "I believe in this case. Let me continue with it."

"Sometimes you must let go of things to have them," Poole said. "You can come to my office with your report and pick up your check."

I needed an employer to continue my investigations, and I asked Veronika if she wanted to buy my services. That's when she told me of her dream. She had seen herself die and then— a figure in a voodoo mask standing over her—come back to life. "I know now that I am one of them," she said. "It was their way of preventing my book. There's nothing anyone can do to help me."

The one hopeful sign was that a single tear moved down her cheek. My zombie lore was limited, though I had never heard of one crying before, which is what I told her. She said she would look at her notes to see if what I said was true. Then she instructed me to tie her to the bed so that the drums would not move her to join the dance of the dead.

I left her trussed to the headboard of my bed and drove through the early morning to Dr. Poole's New Wave Therapy clinic, the subterranean sound of the drums in my head as I went, feeling unaccountably drawn by them.

When I arrived at the clinic I was struck by the fact that almost all of the people waiting to see the doctor in his anteroom had minimal affect, which gave me cause for concern. Did the estimable Dr. Poole draw his clientele from the living dead, or was his business with them far more sinister than that?

I didn't wait to be escorted into Poole's office but forced my way in, waving a gun as if it were my ticket to ride. Poole was as gracious as ever, but I could tell he was dissembling.

I could dissemble too—it was not a skill limited only to the rich and powerful—and I asked if I might look at the notes Veronika had taken during her field trip to Haiti.

"Not to worry," he said, writing me a check for twice my arranged fee, dismissing me with a gesture of the hand. "I will give my wife the best care New Wave science can provide."

I almost trusted him, but touched by an intuitive suspicion, a residue of my lost self, I showed my gun and insisted on seeing Veronika's notes. It was the habit of my profession to see one's cases through to the end.

Poole had a moment of panic, his eyes darting around the room as if there were something invisible watching us, but then he shrugged, opened a drawer in his desk and handed me a much-folded newspaper clipping, which was a report of Veronika's death during an anthropological dig in Haiti. The room reeled for me. So Veronika's dream had correspondence in the real world. "This is not exactly in your field of expertise, is it?" Poole sneered.

It was at that moment that Veronika in one of her zombielike trances entered the room. Instinctively, we both moved to her side. "I brought her back," Poole said. "What you see is the price we've both had to pay."

"I think you wanted her this way," I said. "I think she was planning to leave you, and this was the only way you could get to keep her." I looked to Veronika for confirmation, but she seemed unaware of me, was playing in some atavistic way with the doctor's cigarette lighter. Suddenly the papers on Poole's desk burst into flames, the flames extending to the doctor's clothing and then to the walls of the room. Poole, who seemed to be melting, huddled in a corner of the room, swatting at his clothing.

In the confusion that followed, I lifted Veronika in my arms and escaped from the burning building. Various zombie types followed us in their lumbering, determined way, but eventually I got us into my car and drove off, a few pursuers hanging on, then falling away.

We fled San Francisco in my rented Imperial and headed north, plugs in our ears to shut out the siren call of the drums. "I can't leave," she repeated a few times, but then she relaxed and closed her eyes.

Certain nightmare hallucinations appeared before us from time to time, serpents with human heads, children in Nazi uniforms, fire storms, the disembodied vampire head of an actor who had been a former president of the United States, nuclear flashes, though I kept going, refusing to accept their authority over our lives.

"We must be a danger to them," Veronika said. "Or why would they keep after us?"

I had no answer to her question, thought perhaps it had to do with some remote persistent trace of humanity we had retained and they had lost.

Eventually we reached Seattle where our odd somnambulistic condition seemed less conspicuous than elsewhere.

Linus Poole, who I never thought I'd see again, was squatted in an arm chair in our hotel room, waiting for us.

After giving a demonstration of his power to evoke the spirits of the evil dead, he said he would spare me the worst of the torments he had planned for me if I gave up Veronika to him without resistance.

I took a few minutes to think about it, but my decision had been made from my first pursuit of Veronika (sidestepping awkwardly after her across an open field as she flew overhead) on the first day of the case. I turned Poole down, offered him my soul in place of hers. Then Veronika said she would go with Poole if the detective, meaning me, would be allowed to leave the hotel unharmed. In that moment it seemed my lost soul returned to me. This must be the power of love, I thought, and then almost everything I had forgotten came rushing back to me in profusion.

I remembered that I had once been in love with an older woman, my first wife's mother, Marianna (who had once been married to Linus Poole), an inexplicable fascination that brought torment to everyone touched by it, and after that I was briefly involved with my boss's daughter, Marie, who had a penchant for men with disabling deformities, which led to a fascination with another older woman, Countess Maria Moussakka, a creature with an addictive taste for blood which left me the fading reflection of myself and into a period of convalescence which led to my becoming a theoretical scientist following the brilliantly amoral Dr. Y to Primavera Island to assist him with his experiments in the nature of evolution, all of which came to a bad end, learning only enough from my mistakes to develop my own pointless invention, a time-deforming machine that cost me my job and my reputation, and so I went off on another expedition, this one commanded by the devious impressario Bill Bucks, who abducted (with my complicity) a giant noble ape—both of us in love with the same woman—from a prehistoric island, which led to the beginning of my movie career, and shortly after that, because of Bucks' enmity, the temporary end, returning to San Francisco as an investment banker, meeting someone—this part still a small glimmer in a great fog—on a flight back from Paris, to whom I told the story of the above, and then being wounded and losing my memory, waking up in a hospital with the nagging sense that someone was waiting for me, then finding myself back in San Francisco in the private investigation business, running into Veronika Kay again, who had saved me from the Countess Maria Moussakka, though neither of us recognized the other except in some subterranean unspoken way that somehow transcended memory.

Poole staggered backwards, his hands over his face as if some invisible shaft of light were blinding him. He backed out of the door without opening it, seemed to melt into the distance.

A few moments after the evil Poole's departure, a bluebird settled in the flowerbox outside our window.

We lived together for awhile, Veronika and I, working in a local coffee house that specialized in a decaf hazelnut cappucino with a mocha dusting, pretending to ourselves that living dead were capable of lives just like anyone else.

At night, her tainted soul left her body and flew like a demented bird in the misty rain forest north of the city. I knew that someday she would not return.

twelve

It had been lonely living with Veronika—she was spiritually absent much of the time, but it was even more lonely without her sad spacey semi-presence. Three months after we started living together, she went off one night to follow her stars and was not seen or heard of again. For days on end I imagined her return, imagined hearing her come into the apartment and open the door to our bedroom and approach the bed in her fierce silent way. Of course when I reached for her, which I often did, there were only bed clothes and the absent space she once inhabited.

What was I to believe? I assumed her somnambulism, which seemed in remission during much of our time together, had without warning taken its final toll.

I had been in retirement from the private investigation business, but nothing else I did seemed to occupy me with the same all-consuming satisfaction. My memory was gradually coming back to me, and the more I remembered the more intolerable my life seemed. So when an insurance investigator came to see me about a series of ghostly robberies—my reputation for dealing with the marginally incredible had somehow reached Seattle—I considered coming out of retirement to take a hand in the solution of these uncanny crimes that had thoroughly mystified the police. The investigator, a man of about

77

my own age named Browning who had an offhand manner that inspired trust, presented the details with a certain relish.

At each of the robbery scenes, he said, a single clue had been recovered—a virtually invisible strand of colorless hair, as if it were a calling card. Stop me if you can, the criminal was saying, but don't bet on your chances. All the crimes, which tended to be jewel thefts (only of the tiniest stones), had been committed in daylight, and yet no one had actually seen the thief. The police, after two false arrests, two indictments that got struck down by the courts, had lost interest in the case.

I had the sense on no evidence but intuition that the phantom robber was a woman and that she had a temperament similar to my own. I took the case not so much to catch the thief, but to find out what grim mischance had reduced this brilliant woman to the necessity of crime.

When I wasn't pursuing the case of "The Woman of No Color," I was grieving over Veronika's disappearance, sometimes confusing these two all-consuming obsessions. And there was something else at the back of my memory—an obscure obligation, remote and seemingly unattainable—awaiting my conflicted attention.

The woman did not steal the jewels for themselves, I decided, but as barter for something else. What was it she needed? I asked myself. She needed a drug, which was probably extremely rare, that would give her back her color. I worked out the following scenario.

A woman, probably a scientist, is driving through the night on a desolate winding road in a moonlit woods. She is distracted by some pleasure or discontent, only partly focused at what she is doing. Suddenly, lights appear from the opposite direction—a truck is coming toward her. Truck and car swerve away from what seems an inescapable collision. Nevertheless her car goes out of control and plummets down an embankment, turning over and over as it readies itself for some final reckoning.

The woman wakes in a hospital, all her color gone, her hair whitish, her memory in disrepair. Her illness, the doctor tells her, is extremely rare—there are only two other cases of it on record. To stay alive, she must take regular doses of little known Serum X which has all kinds of side effects, the serum in short supply and therefore inordinately expensive.

*

A life of crime, in which she might employ her freaky absence of color to elude the police, was the only course of action left the poor creature. Her survival was at issue.

What I didn't know and would discover later was that she had two confederates, hospital employees, who had a place north of the city, an unscrupulous older couple looking for the main chance.

Each of the hi-tech shops our woman of no color had robbed had black and white interiors, the kind of background that made her invisible. I anticipated the scene of her next crime and told Browning, making him promise there would be no police and no unnecessary violence. Browning broke faith with our agreement, and the place was crawling with plain-clothes gorillas when I got there. An experienced crook would have read the scene and walked away, but our thief was either desperate or thought she was invincible.

No one saw her go in, but the loot, which had its own visible presence, gave her away as she left the building. A barrage of gunfire which hit everything within a two hundred yard radius also hit its target. I followed the trail of barely visible blood to a white van, the driver, whom I figured to be her accomplice, dressed like a hospital orderly. I followed the van in my car and arrived at a small private hospital calling itself the Windfall Retreat. The place looked deserted when I arrived, as if none of the regular clientele were retreating there at the moment.

I stopped a woman coming out, and I asked her what kind of illnesses the hospital treated. "Unusual ones," she said, hurrying by me.

Where most hospitals were painted white inside, the Retreat had a pitch-black interior. Dressed in black with coal dust on my face and hands, I was able to slip into the small hospital without being noticed.

The transparent blood drops outside her door revealed our thief's room to me. When I entered the room I saw nothing. It took an adjustment of the eyes to pick up her transparent form under a white sheet in the white bed. My purple shadow on the wall provided the only color in the sterile room.

My quarry was indeed a woman as I had conjectured, though so pale she was barely visible even when you knew she was there. She let out a sigh when I appeared, seemed to know me, while, in what amounted to a willed blindness, I had virtually no sense of having seen her before. "Are you all right?" I asked. "Has someone treated your wound?"

And then suddenly she began to fade before my eyes and for a moment I was staring at something that had no presence. As I reached out my hand to her, someone came up from behind and hit me over the back of the head. The last words I remembered hearing were, "Leave him to me."

I woke to find myself lying on the floor, my head in the lap of the wraithlike woman, who was barely visible to me despite our proximity. I realized after a moment, my hair damp with her blood, that her wound had not been treated.

"I'll get one of the doctors to look after you," I said. "You shouldn't let that wound go untended."

"Don't worry about me," she said. "Besides there are no real doctors in this hospital. And anyway it's too late."

The serum that insured her temporary survival, she told me, was administered by the behind-the-scenes administrator of the hospital for whom she stole in order to stay alive.

The police, with their usual self-righteous clamor, were at the door, my dishonorable friend Browning with them. They had captured the thief's accomplices, the driver of the van and his wife who was a defrocked nurse, and had apprehended a hospital van parked outside filled with most of the loot from the most recent phantom robbery. What remained was the apprehension of the woman who had masterminded the crimes.

Which meant, I realized, that I was the only one in the room who could see her. "She must be miles from here by now," I said. And Browning, audacious to a fault, winked at me after corroborating my report.

Stooped over, claiming to have injured my back, I carried the invisible woman out the door and past the unsuspecting police, propping her up in the passenger seat of my car. "Hang on," I said to her. "I'll get help."

She seemed to moan my name, or a name almost mine, in some fever dream. How could she know my name? I wondered. I drove off into the night on a narrow winding country road toward the house of a doctor I knew, a lone police car trailing us. "Watch out for....," she whispered, the unintelligible name she spoke dying in her throat.

As we sped along, she revived long enough to tell me her story, confirming at least half of my guesses as to the nature of her illness and treatment. We were less than a mile from my doctor friend's place when she died in the third clause of a complex sentence that remained permanently unfinished. She was about to give me the name of the man who had traded his life-sustaining serum for the jewels she would risk her life to bring him. As she was in the throes of dying, her original color gradually returned and I was granted, briefly and hopelessly, a full and terrible recognition. The woman without color was Veronika Kay, which meant Browning, who had been playing a double game, was in conspiracy with someone who knew Veronika from another life.

I parked at the side of the road, and after a moment of inconsolable grief—all my losses threading my heart as one—I carried the woman of no color from the car, a woman I had once loved and had lost twice, restored in death to her former self, into the starless night.

thirteen

My success at solving the phantom jewel thefts brought me an endless stream of new cases, delaying the trip east I was bent on making. I would take on three more cases, I decided, the most difficult and challenging available, then I would pack my two suiter and head back to New York in the idle hope of recovering the piece of my life I had lost. The first case I accepted, which concerned a cross-dressing serial killer, took a year out of my life—four months to uncover the killer and twice that amount of time to recover from the process.

Perhaps it was the method I employed to get close to the serial killer that made the solution of the case so ultimately disabling. I had a talent for getting into the mind set of men who killed not for material gain but out of obsessive necessity. By coming to identify with the killer, I was able to anticipate his next move and thereby find him and stop him. The side effects of the method, as well as my encounters with these dangerous madmen, tended to leave me afterwards in physical and emotional disrepair.

The first such killer I encountered had five violent murders of beautiful women under his belt when the case was presented to me. I studied the bodies of the victims and the details of the crimes for seven sleepless nights. And then ...click...click...click...a fluorescent light went on over my head. There was something about the killings—the slashings near the heart that never touched the heart—that led me to believe the killer was a psychiatrist.

Of the five victims, two had been patients of the same doctor, a man named Simon Waters, who had a distinguished practice in Belleview, a posh suburb of Seattle. I went to visit the shrink pretending to be a neurotic in need of his counselling. I was going completely on instinct, and about halfway through our session, fire alarms went off in my head. The doctor chewed on his words as if they were some kind of gourmet experience, tasting his advice to me as if it nourished him. That alone might have been sufficient, but when I noticed he kept a bronzed human finger on his desk, it made me all but certain that he was my man.

I should have realized that while I was reading him, Dr. Waters, who had made a career of deconstructing the soul, was also reading me. He excused himself after our fifty minutes were up to get his appointment book so he might arrange another visit. His nurse, he said, kept his appointments for him. I was unwary, expected nothing but what was promised, was sitting in my chair with my eyes half-shut considering how I might get him to reveal his true nature when without warning a six-foot nurse came at me with a large knife in her hand. I knew without a doubt, even as my life was in the balance, that Waters' true nature had just made itself known.

Having for some time force-marched in the underbrush of Waters' imagination, I had my own knife out moments later and traded him slash for slash. When the police found us and got us to a hospital we were both a mess and from all accounts unrecognizable as our former selves. The odd thing was I was taken for the slasher and he for the victim, and it took a two month trial (after our prolonged recovery) to separate truth from delusion.

Ultimately Waters was unmasked as Linus Poole—it was the one thing I hadn't seen—and sent to a home for the criminally insane. At the same time, I retired, a casualty of my own methods, to a home for the righteous unstable.

Six months and many physical and emotional scars later, when the head of homicide in San Francisco, Harry Monet, a former brother-in-law, asked me to take a hand in another serial murder case, I immediately turned him down. I was still having recurring nightmares from my encounter with Waters. Harry took my refusal as negotiable and fed me the details of what he called the "when push comes to shove murders"—the killer having thrown a succession of people out of high-story windows. When I learned that a friend of mine, the therapist who had seen me through the last ordeal, was the latest victim, the solution to these crimes became an issue of personal vendetta to me.

A succession of marginal high-profile celebrities, all of whom had been interviewed recently on television, had been lured on various pretexts to the top floors of high buildings and had been subsequently thrown out of open windows, or in one case pushed off a roof, to their certain deaths. The killer never struck from the same building twice, which had made it difficult for the police to stake him out.

I was accessing the local TV newscast while sorting and analyzing data on my computer concerning victims of the "High Window Quarterback," as he was known in the tabloids, when I heard my name in the air. An investigative television reporter named Lulu Waller was attacking my appointment as Special Investigator to the police force. She had unearthed a ton of material on me, that, stripped of context, seemed pretty damning. A scary picture of me taken right after my fight with Waters was on the screen with the caption, "Would you want this man helping you across the street?" beneath. Then she said that the evidence indicated that I was a dangerous sociopathic personality. She concluded her presentation with, "In some cases, the cure turns out to be worse than the disease and, when all the evidence is in, this cure may turn out to be the disease itself."

Now I had always been an admirer of Lulu Waller's hard-hitting style, so I was particularly aggrieved to find myself the subject of one of her attacks. The first thing I did was call Harry and resign my post, but Harry said he still had faith in me and refused my resignation. The second thing I did was confront Lulu Waller at the TV station parking lot and ask for an opportunity to give my side of the story.

She grudgingly invited me inside her steel and glass hi-tech loft apartment and interviewed me on closed circuit television, rehearsing new charges among the old. We got into a shouting match in which we each said a string of unforgivable things about the other, then ended up in the missionary position on her couch, our images as we fucked flickering on the screen behind us. It was while we were smoking cigarettes that I learned that she was the same Lulu I had been married to over twenty years ago, Marianna Poole's sexy teenaged daughter. I was saddened to learn that her mother, whom I had once loved, was in jail for killing her second husband after he had betrayed her with a much younger woman, a woman the same age or younger than Lulu herself.

"This doesn't change anything," Lulu said afterwards as I was putting my clothes on to leave. "I've been in love with murderers before."

"I know the feeling," I said.

To get in touch with the killer's psyche, I simulated his performance, pushing a succession of lifelike dummies out of high windows. What does the killer get out of it? I asked myself. What do I get out of it? Does the son-of-a-bitch watch the flight of the body as it falls to its death? If he stayed around to watch, I reasoned, someone would have discovered him by now. No, it was the flight in the imagination (perhaps the killer was even afraid of heights) that excited him. Gradually, I felt myself getting in touch. The killer imagined (as I did) that he was the one who was falling. He fell (each murder an attempted suicide) and he survived, which renewed him.

As an experiment, I dressed a dummy in my own clothes and pushed it from the roof of a downtown building. In that moment, I sensed the pleasure the killer derived from his crimes, the secret necessity that drove him from one victim to the next. Perhaps in another dream, I had been such a man myself.

Shadowy shots of my throwing the dummy from the roof appeared on that night's TV newscast. In a live interview, Harry Monet announced that I was no longer working for the San Francisco police. Someone had been following me with a TV camera or had been anticipating my every move in an attempt to discredit me.

They would have to put me under lock and key to stop me from further investigation. The case meant too much to me at this point, had traced itself on my inner life.

If the murders represented a kind of survived suicide, then the victims the killer chose were people with whom he (or she) felt strong identification. I did a collective profile of the four known victims (I had the sense these crimes had been going on in different parts of the country for years), focusing on what they had in common as opposed to what they didn't. They were all awkwardly ambitious, misguided, obsessive people. It was my theory that the killer shared these traits with his (or possibly her) victims, so I threw the names of apparent suspects and non-suspects into the computer to see where the finger pointed. The potential suspects, a list which extended to thirteen, included Lulu, Peter Price, Bill Bucks, Dr. Simon Waters, who was locked away in a home for the criminally insane, Harry Monet, and also, inescapably, myself.

Following an intuition, I went to see Simon Waters (aka Linus Poole) in his cell at the San Francisco Retreat for the Criminally Insane.

Waters was, as always, sly and enigmatic, wanted to know what if anything he stood to gain by sharing his superior acumen with me.

I was of course in no position to offer him anything, since I was working now in an unofficial capacity, though I asked him what he had in mind. "I want to hear the details of your worst nightmare," he said and laughed his hissing laugh. "If it amuses me, I will tell you where and when our pushy killer will strike next."

I had a dream last night of falling from a high building, I told him, from which I woke or seemed to wake in handcuffs, two detectives standing over me with their guns drawn. They took me to the edge of the parapet and showed me spread-eagled below the body of a man who looked enough like me to be my twin. Then they dragged me off to jail, the silent crowd parting like the Red Sea to let me pass.

Waters listened with evident pleasure, nodding from time to time. "You've just dreamed the solution to the murder," he said. "There's no peace in this life for a man like you."

I had no idea what he meant. "You promised me where and when," I said.

"If I did, I did," he said. "Tomorrow night is when. You already know where." Then he turned his back to me and refused to say another word.

The next night, I hung out in the shadows of the roof of a new high-rise building and waited expectantly, my disappointment echoing with each passing hour. Then I remembered that in my dream there was music coming from inside the building, an aria from *Don Giovanni*, and I knew in a flash that the roof of the opera house was the venue for the high-window quarterback's next indecency.

A handful of people were still exiting the opera house when I got there and I slipped in, pretending to be an employee, and climbed the winding stairs to the roof. I was almost too late, a life and death struggle going on between two shadowy figures on the parapet of the domed roof as I emerged. Just as I reached them, the two figures, disconcerted by my sudden presence, lost their balance and fell, letting go of one another to grasp some tenuous purchase on the protective ledge. I was there in time to grab each of them by a hand, Harry Monet and Lulu Waller, killer and victim (but which was which?), holding on with all the strength I had while waiting for help which never seemed to arrive. After twenty minutes or so, my arms began to ache, and I faced the dilemma of choosing between them.

The decision made itself when Harry slipped from my grasp and fell. I was able to save Lulu, using two hands to pull her back onto the parapet. Semi-failure in my book doesn't account itself success. And though Harry's fall may have been a kind of poetic justice, it was all I could do to keep myself from following my former brother-in-law's flight into the void.

All that was left was the sorting out of who did what to whom. Having no other eye-witness story, I took Lulu's version of what happened on faith, and let the case solve itself. She and Harry, she said, had been secretly married, which had made it difficult for her to see clearly what was in front of her eyes, namely that Harry had taken the law into his own hands. Loyalty had corrupted her judgment. Harry, who had a fear of heights, had been the high-window quarterback, seeing it as a sidelight of his job to rid the city of its malcontents. When she had discovered the truth, just hours before I found them together, and confronted Harry with it, he promised to give up "his calling," as he called it, if she promised not to give him away. "As a reporter, it is my sacred trust to give the public what it wants," she told him. I had apparently arrived on the scene the moment after Harry had coaxed Lulu to the roof's edge and was trying to air mail her to the street below.

"Nothing is ever over when it's over, is it?" she said ruefully.

*

For weeks after that I climbed to the roof of every high building in town and wondered how it would feel to fly off into space. Lulu sometimes followed me and threw her arms around me from behind, but I had no intention of jumping, not then, not yet. I just wanted the bad dreams to go away. This was my last look into the void, I told myself each time I stood at the edge and imagined the frozen seconds of the final flight.

fourteen

I never seemed to get from point A to point B without some unanticipated detour leading me astray. The death of Harry Monet weighed on me, and I drove at a furious pace as if outrunning the torment that pursued. After awhile, giving way to distraction and loss of purpose, I moved fecklessly from city to city, going wherever circumstance led me, trying on new names and new careers, sleeping in cheap motels and the back seats of cars, trading in one car, one career, one life after another as though in shedding those false skins, I was somehow getting closer to my real self. Occasionally a letter from Lulu Waller would find me, which was difficult to figure since I had left no forwarding addresses. I collected her letters, or let them collect, planning to read them at some undefined point in the future which never seemed to arrive, the letters piling up at the bottom of my suitcase, amnesiac memorabilia. They remained, the unopened letters, a potential source of contact with another human voice.

Then there was my own voice which nattered on accusingly in my head. I had been running from that voice and had been unsuccessful in shaking it. I thought maybe if I forced myself to listen to others, if I had to concern myself with strangers, I could escape that rueful interior voice, so I set up shop as a psychotherapist for a while in Denver, Colorado. One of

89

the more established shrinks in the area, Dr. Henrietta Hillyard, agreed to pass on the cases she couldn't or wouldn't handle herself. The odd and the marginal danced their concerns through the door to my office. For the following year until it was time to move on, I became resident therapist to the local untouchables.

One day a blond man, a little over five feet tall, came into my office, wearing a full length black cape of a sort that was no longer in style. He refused to sit in the facing chair or lie down on the couch on the other side of the room until I heard his story. He had grown up, he said, in an orphanage in Hong Kong, an occidental in an oriental world, and had been considered backward and feeble by his guardians. For reasons that were partially ironic, his schoolmates had nick-named him "Three Feet of Fury." He aspired to be a warrior, read biographies of famous warriors, engendered warrior thoughts, practiced on the sly the craft that had chosen him in his intuitive, untutored, and, as he put it, three-footed way.

On my patient's 16th birthday, a famous blind warrior named Noyo visited the orphanage to give a demonstration of his martial artistry and to find if possible—this was his unannounced agenda—his predestined apprentice.

I was tempted to interrupt Sumgun, which was the only name he offered, to ask him if he had ever been treated for delusional episodes before, but his sincerity was so evident I decided to hear him out before passing judgment.

Noyo proposed a hand-to-hand combat session with the strongest boy in the orphanage, Sumgun continued, and the head teacher offered the resident martial arts champ, a mean-spirited swaggering bully known as Lout-si as opponent. The bully Lout-si surveyed the aged, flu-ridden blind warrior and he saw it as an opportunity to demonstrate his superiority. Disrespecting the famous old warrior, he swaggered from side to side, daring Noyo to lay a hand on him. In the blink of an eye—even in decrepitude, the blind warrior moved faster than the eye could record—Lout-si was disabled and thrown through the gymnasium wall. Lout-si's second arrogant try met with a similar fate. No one else would take the challenge (Sumgum offered himself but they said he was too feeble), and the blind warrior left the orphanage in sorrow and disappointment.

Walking in the woods in his usual meditative state, Noyo was set upon by a group of his ancient enemies disguised as

bandits. He dismembered the first three with one of his pat-
ented lightning strokes, but the fourth tripped him from behind
and was about to kill the warrior when Sumgun jumped out of
his hiding place (he had been following Noyo) and karate-
kicked the bandit into the trees with his hidden leg.

"You are the apprentice my dream has promised me," said
Noyo, who talked like some guy in a comic book. "Are you
prepared to give up all human endeavor to become a famous
warrior?" Sumgun said, "Sure."

They had some cool times together, Sumgun said, roam-
ing the woods, fighting off bandits and the like, but Noyo was
getting too old for the life. So they moved to southern California where the blind warrior set up a school for the training of
famous warriors, his entire life savings tied up in the enterprise. Sumgun was his assistant and number one student,
though he would have traded away the honor to be back on
the road again. Noyo insisted that he still had much to learn.

They were making a modest success of the enterprise,
when a rival school, bigger and better financed, governed by
the most evil of Noyo's ancient enemies, opened across the
street. The intent, it soon became clear, was to put Noyo out
of the education business. The apprentice warriors from the
new school, who had no sense of traditional courtesy, took
every opportunity to threaten and assault the smaller students
from Noyo's school. The worst offender was the bully Lout-
si, who had developed over the years into a powerful and
unscrupulous warrior, someone whose strength apparently pro-
ceeded from the evil side of the warrior soul.

One day, Dr. Horn, the head of the new school, challenged
Noyo to a showdown of warriors, winner take all, which the
blind warrior unaccountably refused. When Sumgun pressed
him for an explanation, he said, "Never fight your enemy when
he is awake and you are under bed covers with eyes pasted
shut."

A follow-up challenge was issued from the new school,
champion against champion in combat to the death, which
meant Lout-si against whoever took up the gauntlet. Sumgun
accepted against Noyo's wishes, creating a rift in their friendship.

At the local bookmaking and opium house, which kept a
few washing machines up front for show, Lout-si was established as a ten to one favorite. Sumgun relished the position

of underdog, though he might have preferred the negative odds to be less prohibitive.

He trained day and night to ready himself for the competition, and he truly believed, no matter the odds against him, that he would emerge the victor. That was before his girlfriend Flower was kidnapped by Lout-si's supporters, and he was warned that she would be killed, dismembered petal by petal, if he won the combat. He found himself caught in a moral dilemma. Was there more honor in winning the match and losing Flower or in losing like a dog so that Flower might be spared? Not knowing how to answer the question or what to do, he turned to Noyo for advice. "Have eyes in your heart," Noyo told him, "teeth in your fingers, and fire in your shoes."

Noyo, who had seen the place of Flower's imprisonment in a vision, promised to find her for his protégé and bring her back alive. "If you do not give your heart in combat," he added, "your warrior soul will leave your body and hide like pond scum in your enemy's hot tub."

Nevertheless, Sumgun remained conflicted. He slept badly and trained in a dispirited way as the moment of warrior truth approached.

True to his promise, Noyo put on his old robes and went off in the dead of night to rescue Flower in a ten year old Chevrolet he had never driven before. This was the night before the day before Sumgun was to fight Lout-si, and he had no knowledge of Noyo's effort until word reached him that the blind warrior had been arrested by the police for driving on the wrong side of the road without a California license. It was all in Sumgun's hands now. What he didn't know was that the cops who had arrested the famous blind warrior were dishonorable men in the pay of Dr. Horn. He tried to bail Noyo out, but they set the blind warrior's bail at a price beyond his reach.

As Sumgun was leaving the prison, caught up in the confusion of his present difficulties, he was fair game for the three thugs in Horn's employ who ambushed him. Before he could take their measure, he had the kneecap broken on one of his legs, two black eyes and a shoulder separation. It was all he could do to drag himself back to his small room at the back of the school. He knew he had no chance to win in his deteriorated condition, but he made his way to The Stadium of Dreams the next morning, his damaged leg trussed up in an Ace bandage, determined to make an honorable effort. He was twenty minutes late, arriving in time to hear an announcement over the loudspeaker, alleging that he had refused to fight out of cowardice.

His presence caused a hopeful stir among the large crowd, and it saddened him to know he could only disappoint his loyal supporters.

Using a variety of dirty tricks, including sand in the face, the villainous Lout-si mocked Sumgun in the early going, embarrassed and tormented him while setting him up for the kill. On the verge of humiliating defeat, Sumgun had a vision of Flower's elegant face. In the vision, Flower pleaded with him to win. He took heart from her words and blocked a potentially fatal karate chop to the back of his neck. And then in an inspired moment, he got off one of his flying three-footed kicks (ignoring the pain of his multiple injuries), which drove Lout-si to the far reaches of the stadium.

Moments after his uncelebrated victory, with Noyo as his guide, he rushed off to the warehouse where Flower was held captive. Delayed by traffic and a Fourth of July parade, they arrived too late and found Flower dead with a note pinned to her chest. "Death visited here," it said.

He didn't remember the details of what happened after that, except the evidence indicated that in his fury he had reduced to rubble everything in his path, including the entire population of the new school, among them the sinister Dr. Horn who had turned himself into a toothless dog to escape Sumgun's fury.

All would have been well had Flower lived to share his victory, and in the aftermath of his vengeance, he was inconsolable. He told Noyo of his grief, and the old warrior prayed to the warrior Gods to turn back the clock and thereby restore Flower to sentience. Somehow this prayer was answered— Sumgun didn't know at the time what Noyo had promised in exchange—and all was as it had been. Except that Dr. Horn and Lout-si had become sweet-natured and peace was made between the two schools and they toasted each other and smoked the pipe and caroused through the night, celebrating the reconciliation of the two opposing camps.

"So the story ends happily," I said, not sure at this point why he had come to see me.

"Happily? No!" he said. "My moment of glory had been

wiped out, and in all these years I have never had another such opportunity. I was meant to be a warrior, and there was no longer anyone left to fight in anger. Married life didn't agree with my disposition, and Flower left me after three years to live with Lout-si, who had become like a brother to me. I've forgotten my fury, doctor. I'm a broken man with nothing in his life but peace and contentment. I want the old ways returned, the days of war and glory. I have become nothing but a toothless dog."

"You must learn to accept things as they are," I said. "In the real world, you cannot repeat the past more than once or twice."

Then he let out an ear-shattering cry and lifted the skirt of his cape, revealing his dreaded third leg, which went into action almost immediately, silencing my disbelief. In a matter of minutes, he smashed everything in my office, and I could see from where I cowered in a corner, pleased at what I had accomplished, that "Three Feet of Fury" was himself again.

fifteen

After three sessions of transactional therapy, the diminutive Sumgun seemed to regain his zest for violent living, which brought me some favorable word of mouth. My growing reputation as a miracle man was a mixed blessing, bringing me more patients than I could possibly take on and alienating a number of my more traditional colleagues. Even my friend, Henrietta Hillyard, who had referred a number of patients to me, let me know that she thought some of my methods were fundamentally unsound. Nevertheless she sent me Euphoria Heller, a hard drinking, former Miss America runner-up, who had been a patient of hers for two years, to get a second opinion on what had become an increasingly strange case.

The problem started five months ago when Euphoria woke up in some marginally famous game-show host's kingsize bed, unable to remember how she got there or, until she saw his face, the identity of the negligible celeb seemingly lost in sleep next to her. About the time she discovered who the guy was, she also discovered that he was stone dead and more than probably murdered. She had had a similar experience the week before, so it concerned her that an unpleasant pattern was beginning to emerge. "Am I doing this to myself?" she asked herself in her more sober moments. "What's going on?"

*

She couldn't imagine that she had killed the man, which was what she told Dr. Hillyard, but then again she seemed to have some kind of black-out problem, leaving large chunks of her day (and night) unaccounted for. The inevitable question came up: Was it possible to kill someone and not remember a thing about it the morning after?

"That's an area that might be fruitful to explore further," Hillyard told her. "The human mind has an infinite capacity for evasion and so forth."

Well, the more they explored the subject, the less certainty Euphoria had about anything. It was almost better to believe that she had been killing these men unwittingly, she thought, than to be mired in uncertainty.

I heard her out in a sympathetic manner without making a judgment one way or another. When Dr. Hillyard called to ask my opinion, I said I didn't know whether she was killing her bedfellows or not, but I believed that that she believed in her own innocence. I said I would be interested in further commerce with her.

Euphoria came to see me again a week later with a similar story. A few days after our first session, she was alone at home taking a nap (after a few drinks), waking three hours later to find another vaguely familiar celebrity in blood-stained unwakeable sleep in bed next to her. It turned out to be the exhibitionistic millionaire owner of several local sports teams.

Spooked by the apparent behavior of her hidden self, she had fled her apartment and had not returned. What should she do? she asked me. The evidence against her was overwhelming.

The evidence was too overwhelming, I said, for me to accept it at face value, and I suggested she hold out, if she could, a few more days. So I found her a place to hide, a small cabin in the woods, and offered my services (as a detective) in helping her find the real murderer, which was something she needed to do before the police, who had glommed on to her as their main suspect, made their pounce.

What I didn't know was that, having discovered another marginally familiar dead man in her bed in the cabin in the woods—it was a stand-up comic this time—she began to wonder if I might not be the murderer myself. So when I called to say I was coming out to the cabin to bring her food—I settled on an egg salad sandwich—Euphoria hightailed out of there, making arrangements on the phone with Henrietta for a place to bunk.

When I arrived at the cabin, the only one there to receive my sandwich was a man who had lost his appetite forever. I knew immediately why Euphoria had gone, and I had a strong suspicion where. There were more surprises, not all of which I anticipated, waiting for me at the turn in the road.

When Euphoria arrived at Henrietta's apartment, the place was dark except for flashes of light sent off by the neon sign of the all-night diner across the street. All the lights were off, the apartment a mass of undefinable shadows. When she turned on a light, she found Henrietta sitting in a chair across from her, stripes of shadow imprisoning her face. "The police will be here in ten minutes," the therapist said in her characteristic monotone. "I want to tell you why I called them before they arrive so you won't feel betrayed."

"I'm getting the hell out of here," Euphoria said, making no move to leave. "You think I'm the murderer, don't you?"

"It seems odd, doesn't it," Henrietta said, "that someone seems willing to kill all these not-quite famous people just to get you in trouble. If that were the case, one murder would be sufficient, wouldn't it? Five corpses does seem like overdoing it, wouldn't you say?"

At that moment I slipped into Henrietta's apartment, having come on a hunch, having no idea what I hoped to discover.

Euphoria had her finger pointed at Henrietta. "Hey, wait a minute," she said. "How did you know there were five? I never told anyone five."

A long silence followed. "You did, of course," she said. "You just don't remember. It's the blackout problem all over again, don't you see? The memory obliterates what it can't bear to remember."

"No!" Euphoria shouted as if guns were trained on her and about to fire, abruptly collapsing on the floor in a faint. It was more trance than faint, and her eyelids fluttered as she lay on the floor reliving pieces of her childhood her memory had for years refused to tolerate.

Shock had unearthed her buried past. She was a little girl again (this told to me later on), and her mother was entertaining a famous actor in the living room of their small apartment.

The actor, who had been drinking heavily, dragged her mother against her will into the bedroom while Euphoria and her older sister, Etta, watched. Her mother was pleading with the actor to stop, but he seemed determined to get his way. "Get mother's gun," the older sister said to her, and she did, she got the gun, which she handed over to her sister. One of them—she's never been quite sure which one—fired the gun at the actor, but her mother got in the way. Her mother collapsed to the floor, a corsage of blood just below her decolletage. The actor fled the house, or would have, had not a second shot brought him to his knees and a third brought down the curtain on a limited run. She tried to scream, but she was mute. Her sister handed her the gun and made her promise not to tell anyone what had happened.

In the second memory, she was with a man in a shadowy room; they were drinking heavily, passing a bottle between them. Another figure was there—just out of view, wearing a black veil. Then she was in bed with the man, rolling around, smothered momentarily by his weight. "The category you've chosen is sexual dalliance," the man said. Out of the shadows came a gloved hand holding a gun. An explosion woke her. "Watch out, mother," a voice (hers or her sister's) called. The warning came too late. The figure in the bed with her was beyond salvation.

When Euphoria regained consciousness, she found herself sitting in a chair, one of her wrists cuffed to a spindly armrest. I was in the room at this point, standing among the police who were in the process of making an arrest.

"Isn't it strange," Euphoria said in a dreamy voice. "All this time I had a sister I didn't know I had."

The assertion electrified the room. "Do you know where this sister is?" I asked her.

Moments after the question floated in the air, circumstances answered it. Henrietta had a gun in her hand and was backing out of the room. "Don't trouble yourself about me," she said when we noticed her impending exit. "I'll just go away."

"Euphoria's not taking the rap for you this time," I said.

"You know nothing," she shrieked at me and fired the gun wildly in my direction. Reflexively, the police fired back, and Henrietta went down like a pile of wet wash. Dragging her chair with her along the floor, Euphoria pulled herself to her sister's side for a short-lived reunion.

"I've always hated you, baby," Henrietta reported in her dying breath. "It wasn't personal. The heart evades what it can't bear to know."

As Euphoria offered her forgiveness, I threw open the heavy curtains in the dark room. The shadows vanished, fled across the room like scurrying lizards, and the forbidding and mysterious, touched by the morning light, seemed familiar and ordinary.

That seemed to end the case. The therapy, which had been focused on a specific problem, wound down accordingly, but as it turned out, as it always turns out, there was more to come.

I was summoned one night to Euphoria's place at 2AM—her voice on the phone barely recognizable—and found all the lights out on my arrival, and Euphoria unavailable. I made my way to the bedroom and pulled back the curtains, discovering the body of a man in Euphoria's bed, a once well-known TV anchorman long past his prime, a bullet hole the size of a doll's eye in his forehead.

So what was I to believe, what was anyone to believe?

When I turned on the light, Henrietta or a woman who looked like Henrietta, smoking gun in her lap, was sitting in a rocking chair next to the bed, chanting to herself, "The mind has an infinite capacity for self-deception. The mind has an infinite..."

I didn't stay around this time for the post-mortem, or the completion of her reiterated sentence, but fled in dismay from her house, starting up my car before the seat belt was in place, then tearing off with a screech of the wheels, on a winding road which led to other roads and then to an interstate highway, calling the police from the first gas station I passed, telling them where to go and what they might find. Pursuing salvation in distance, I would not stop again until lack of sleep or fuel demanded I pull off the road and gather myself for the still longer trip ahead.

sixteen

When I got to Chicago, I ran into Lola Monet, who was working as a cabaret singer at Club Panache and we hooked up together for awhile until something out of Lola's past, two things actually, entered our lives and changed them in ways that would have been hard to anticipate or imagine. The first ghost from the past was her first husband, Vladimir, a man who had been a musician in the same orchestra as her father and had married Lola when she was fifteen. Lola had left him when she was twenty-one and he had moved to Europe, where he had established himself as a classical conductor of some note. During the intervening years, Lola had become a fashion model, an anthropologist, a movie actress, my wife, (and recently a cabaret singer). She had tamed the great ape, Prince Dong, and had looked after him during his brief ascendent moment in Hollywood.

She hadn't seen Vladimir for thirteen years when he showed up one night at the cabaret to see her perform. The famous conductor, who was guesting with the Chicago Symphony, went backstage with flowers and champagne, and they talked through the night. A little more than a week later Lola left me—it was an amicable split—to move in with Vladimir. There was someone else that night in the audience, someone she hadn't seen in even longer than thirteen years, who would play a part in our lives, but he didn't announce his presence until somewhat later.

The second man, Pud, who had once worked as a handyman for Vladimir and Lola, and was now a government operative, had also never stopped loving Lola. They had had a brief affair—one or two nights together—during the first difficult year of Lola's marriage to Vladimir, and then he had gone away, had virtually disappeared, at Lola's urging. All of this became known to me after Lola one afternoon had left the suburban house she shared with Vladimir to do some shopping at the local mall and had not returned.

Perceiving me as a friend of the family, Vladimir called me in to investigate Lola's disappearance. The last thing Vladimir wanted was to have the story scandal-mongered around in the supermarket tabloids. I said I would do what I could to keep things quiet, but that finding Lola had to be our first priority.

We sat in his living room, drinking expensive port, trying to make sense of what might have happened. We both came to the conclusion that the kidnapper, if indeed she had been taken against her will, had no intention of returning her. Ransom was not his issue—it was something else.

I tried to put myself in the mindset of someone who would kidnap a woman solely for the purpose of having her in his possession and came to the conclusion that it had to be a thwarted lover, someone who did not take defeat gracefully. The only person I knew who was in that category and was still carrying a torch was me, which made me wonder if Vladimir hadn't hired me to find her because he suspected me of taking her. I asked if I could go through Lola's room to see if there were any clues that might shed some light on what happened, and Vladimir said he intended to protect Lola's privacy even in the face of prolonged absence and possible death. In his view, he said, there were some principles that might not be compromised.

I imagined wanting Lola so much that I would risk everything to have her in my possession, the star acquisition of my private museum, the human butterfly encased behind glass, the beloved as a thing of beauty and joy forever. I spent hours in front of the computer, creating a profile of her kidnapper as if he were a more extreme version of the possessive self I had imagined, and the more I understood him, the more urgent it seemed to find Lola. So when I knew Vladimir was away, I broke into his house and went through Lola's room. Two letters, one written eighteen years ago, one written two days before she vanished, coupled with some entries from her journal, provided me with the information I needed.

Gradually, I pieced together a credible account of what had happened to Lola. A man she knew as Pud—his real name, Alphonse—a young carpenter doing odd jobs for her husband, fell hopelessly in love with her. This was eighteen years ago. Flattered by his devotion, Lola slept with him one night while her husband was out of town. To get Pud to leave, Lola had to promise that she would eventually come back to him. As a symbol of her commitment to him, Lola gave Pud an ankle chain as a parting gift.

Over the years, Lola, who had become an anthropologist and a film star and had lived in domestic harmony with the great ape of Amoranta Island, forgot about her promise to Pud, but Pud never forgot Lola. If anything, his feelings for her, which were exaggerated from the outset, became further intensified by her prolonged absence from his life. When he saw her again at the cafe, he expected her to throw herself into his arms. That she didn't, that she didn't even recognize him, pushed him one step further over the edge. That's probably when the kidnap plan was hatched. His intent was not to harm her but to make her remember that she was his intended, as he was hers.

But where had he taken her? I phoned Vladimir and asked him where he and Lola were living when they were first married, thinking if I were Pud and wanted Lola to love me again, I would take her to the place where we first made love. Vladimir wouldn't talk to me, said he suspected me of breaking into his place and taking some papers from Lola's room, which I of course denied. It took me another few days, but eventually I figured out what I needed to know without Vladimir's cooperation.

Pud, it turned out, had kidnapped Lola in the back of an ice-cream truck, using a drugged creamsicle to render her unconscious.

When she woke up, she found herself in the very cabin on the Oregon coast in which they had once made love eighteen years earlier. The recognition was extremely disorienting, she told me later. They were also, she discovered to her further surprise, chained together at the ankle, each of them with an identical ankle bracelet, his name on hers, hers on his.

For a while, she insisted on being freed, but it only made Pud more possessive and demanding. What he wanted was to return things to the way they had been, to force her to remember that she had once promised to love him forever.

As she became increasingly desperate, she dissembled to try to gain his trust, pretended that she also cared for him, but no matter what she said he would not let her out of his sight, he would not undo the chain. He had gotten it into his head that destiny had brought them together, that some higher power intended it, and he pleaded his case over and over, as if insistence itself might win her. He wore her down, but she held out against him, did whatever she could think of to break his resolve, refusing to wash or do her hair and then refusing to eat the mostly inedible food he lovingly prepared for her.

Every night while Pud slept, the resourceful Lola sawed away at her ankle chain with a nail file. Since Pud slept no more than three hours a night, it took her nine sleepless nights to break through the chain. Exhausted from her ordeal, barely able to walk, she dragged herself to the door, which had several locks that needed undoing, and out of the cottage. It was snowing out—lightly at first, but gradually increasing in intensity—and she had no coat.

When Pud woke and discovered himself unattached, Lola missing from his life, he rushed from the cabin like a man possessed.

I had parked down the road, and I had been going from cabin to cabin showing Lola's photo, when I saw this huge creature in his underwear trudging toward me. Before I could could get Lola's photo from my coat pocket, Pud knocked me over with an arm as thick as a log, and I fell in a ditch, pieces of my life passing before me in incomprehensible profusion.

When I was able to get to my feet—I don't know how much time had passed—I discovered a woman's scarf on the ground outside what looked like a derelict cottage. Gun in hand, I knocked at the door. When no one answered, I tried the door handle, warily opening the unlocked door. As I stepped inside, this huge figure immaculately dressed in a white jacket came rushing at me with an axe that already had blood on its blade. I got off a shot just as the axe grazed my skull, aware of the bullet knicking Pud in the shoulder before fading to black.

When I awoke I had my head in Sassy's lap, but that was just a dream.

When I awoke again I heard music—it was Lola singing—and I followed the sound to a shack in back of the main cottage, which was the place Pud used to stay during his handyman days. There were two slashed bodies in the snow, one was a detective from a rival agency—the other, still alive, was Vladimir.

Lola's voice, I discovered, was coming from a stereo system and, for the moment of that discovery, I gave up hope of ever seeing her alive again. When I entered the building, which was a storage room filled with debris, I saw Lola lying unconscious on a narrow cot, a slash of blood on her forehead. There was no sign of her oversized kidnapper, and I put my ear to her chest and listened to her troubled heart. She was still alive and seemed in fact to be coming around, when Pud, who was seriously wounded, came staggering into the room, the murderous axe still in his possession. I stepped out of his way, but he stumbled against me, both of us losing our balance, the axe flying loose, falling at the foot of Lola's cot.

When Lola called his name, he got to his feet and turned toward her with his arms out like a sleepwalker, moving blindly in her direction. She held the bloody axe out in front of her, and Pud, with what intent it was impossible to know, impaled himself on the blade. Lola gasped, which elicited a grim smile from her fatally wounded lover. In the interim, two policemen had entered and sent some lead in Pud's direction as well as mine, covering all bases. In his last moments, Pud wrapped his huge hands around Lola's ankle chain, establishing connection one last time. The combined strength of the three of us, the two policemen and myself, were insufficient to free Lola from the dead man's possessive grasp, the story of which, with the usual distortions, was plastered across the front pages of the various supermarket scandal magazines as soon as they could get to press.

The magazines further reported that Pud and Lola remained united for five hours after Pud's death, until the police were able to find a tool capable of cutting the steel bracelet from her ankle.

*

I read about Lola and Pud in a hospital bed—I was being treated for a concussion, which had unleashed a series of bad dreams concerning a woman in a hotel room in another city, a woman I had met on a flight from Paris to New York. Her name, it seemed to me, started with an M, and she was half Vietnamese and half-French, and she had sent me on an errand that I seemed hopelessly unable to complete.

seventeen

The day I was supposed to leave the hospital, a man who identified himself as a Mr. Summerfield came to see me and solicited my services for a government organization called The Committee. When I didn't seem particularly eager, he let me know in his affectless way that refusal was not one of my options. If I didn't accept his offer, he would see that I spent the rest of my life in the government's temporary incarceration program. He had the goods on me, he kept insisting, and I thought maybe what he was referring to was something I had blocked from memory. As I later discovered, he had come on to me by mistake—he had confused me with a journalist in the ward on the floor above—but I had no way of knowing that then.

"It would be wasteful of me, wouldn't it, to put you in a padded cell at the taxpayers' expense," he said, "when it would be just as simple, simpler really, to have you disappear. Anyway, Hemmingstein, if that's your real name, every man has an obligation to serve his country when called."

"Someone's waiting for me at the Hotel Paradise," I told him.

"The sooner you get started, Jack, the sooner you'll be able to keep your appointment."

106

*

There was a renegade former government agent, privy to secrets that might embarrass some people in high places, who was believed to be hiding out under an assumed identity in a mental institution in Baltimore, Maryland called the Bent Mind Retreat. My job, assuming I accepted it, was to get committed to this institution, find out who the agent was (no one still alive had ever seen him) and determine how the agent might best be neutralized. An operative (code name: Maribeau), presenting herself as my sister, would come and visit once a week to get my reports.

"What if the person you want isn't in this place?" I asked.

"You'll find him one way or another," said the thin- lipped Summerfield, who had a Wendell Corey smile. "We wouldn't have chosen you if we didn't think you were up to the job."

My scam was that I was delusional and believed I was going into the asylum to write a book on the mentally ill. This would allow me to question patients about their pasts without engendering undue wariness. Spying, I could see, was also a kind of science without redeeming social value.

There were seven people in my ward, and one of them, said my sources, was a former Committee agent, an unscrupulous killer and careerist whose continued survival was a danger to the free world. In my assumed role as delusionary biographer, I found myself the unwitting ear to a succession of heart-rending stories. A man named Quixote, who looked vaguely familiar, told me he had been an actor under another name, highly respected in his craft, until he began to over-identify with the characters he portrayed. He would give himself to a role so absolutely that when the performance was over, he had increasing difficulty returning to real life. He ultimately killed several people, confusing the real folks in his world with the fictions in his movies. "Who are you playing now?" I asked him. "I'm playing a man," he said, "whose sincerity is undeniable." Indeed, his sincerity, a quality difficult to evaluate in a madman or spy, seemed beyond question.

The next one in the ward I was able to get close to was a woman who called herself M. The woman in her late 40s, meticulous, obsessed with washing her hands, affecting a barely perceptible limp, was silent for the first several days of our acquaintance. Once she started to talk, however, once the boundary of restraint between us was broken, she told me all I wanted to know and almost more than I could readily process.

She had been charged, she confided, with murdering her husband's mother, who was also his secret lover, and it had been her lawyer's idea—a man in the pay of her husband—to take an insanity plea. She was also at the time—this a reluctant admission—in love with her husband's brother, whom she said had masterminded the killing. It had been a crime of passion, she insisted, a crime of outrage, and at the same time an unfortunate accident. She was not to blame or not wholly to blame. She had gone to see her mother-in-law not to kill her but to let the unnatural woman know she knew what was going on and would no longer tolerate it. It was the mother-in-law who had produced the gun and in the struggle shot herself. Still, it was not an explanation anyone wanted to believe, which explained the apparent necessity for the insanity plea and lifetime incarceration at the Retreat.

The next day she told me a completely different story, claiming she had been a society heiress, whose husband, a powerful and influential lawyer with political aspirations, had planned to murder her to further his career. She had discovered the plot when a man wearing a hooded mask tried to strangle her. She had shot him through the heart in self-defense. The husband, who had powerful friends, had tampered with the evidence, and so her crime—the man killed was her husband's partner—was made to seem arbitrary and therefore mad.

On the third day, she told me she was a famous Russian aristocrat, a tsarina whom the communists had tried to kill, and that she was hiding out in the Retreat by arrangement with the American government. Each story was told in a quiet reasonable voice, and if there hadn't been three stories, I might have believed any one of them. She remained on my list under the category of "possible though unlikely."

eighteen

The next guy I got to tell me his story was an old coot wearing a grease-stained cowboy hat. He wore a gun belt at all times (even to bed with him at night) and kept a dangerous-looking cap pistol in his holster. The first thing he told me was that he had been a famous gunfighter in his day under the name of Missouri Lightning.

The story he wanted to tell about himself concerned an episode toward the end of his legendary career. He was retired at the time, an undiagnosed injury to his shooting hand, which was his left, having forced him out of the game at the top of his powers. He had to move around a lot and keep his true identity a secret, because if word got out he'd lost the use of his shooting hand, there would be legions of young punks around, looking to take him out.

To maintain his anonymity he had taken a job as a cowboy at a cattle ranch, the largest of its kind in Montana, where he found himself pursued by the owner's wife, Marlena, a former girlfriend who was still carrying a torch for him. So it seemed like more than a coincidence when Missouri's boss, Colonel Warren Wilt, an ambitious power broker, asked him to keep an eye on his wife for him. Marlena tended to work on Missouri's sympathies by telling him stories about the colonel's corrupt practices and general brutality. Why don't you leave

109

him then? he asked her. Because, she said, he'd never let me, he'd kill me first. You know what he's like.

Also working at the ranch was a surly young gunfighter who went under the name Black Pete, a reference to the predominant color of his wardrobe. Pete's father, a major bad guy in his time, was killed years back in a showdown with Missouri, and Pete was still grieving his death. In fact, he had spent most of his young punk life in pursuit of his father's killer, whom he had had described to him but had never knowingly seen.

Meanwhile, Colonel Wilt had been creating a private empire by making life miserable for his neighbors and then buying them out cheap. Wilt owned virtually all the land in and around the town of Wilton, except for a large farm run by a stubborn old man named Patterson, who had refused to be intimidated. The farmer, Piers Patterson, unbeknownst to Missouri, was his lost father, a man he has not seen since he was a silent lonely child of eight.

Wilt was determined—it was his major objective—to take possession of Patterson's spread, and to that end he sent Missouri with three other men to make a final unrefusable offer to old Patterson. One of the cowboys in the negotiating party was Black Pete.

It was at that point that the coot, who was extremely childlike, discontinued his story for the night.

When the story continued the next morning, some of the terms of it had changed. Aware that Missouri had something going with his wife, Wilt sent word to Patterson that he was about to be assassinated by a team of heartless gunfighters. Informed of the danger, Patterson sent out his own nasty guns to bushwhack Missouri and his men before they could reach his farm.

Ambushed, taken completely by surprise, Missouri was left for dead; his charges, except for Black Pete (his life saved by Missouri), were wiped out to a man. Missouri would have died from his wounds if not for the ministrations of a former Sioux princess named Tondelaya, who lived with her aging father in the forest. Using the magical properties of certain herbs known only to her people, she gradually nursed Missouri back to health. They didn't have time to become lovers, though there were some moves in that direction. Missouri gave his word to her on his departure that he would come back for her after his mission of vengeance was completed.

Meanwhile, Wilt, who had more poisonous tricks than a scorpion, incited the new marshall, a man committed to the letter of the law, to bring Patterson and his gunslingers up on charges of unprovoked murder. There were a number of witnesses, including Black Pete (thought to be the only survivor of the massacre), to verify that Wilt's apparent "peace messengers" had been ambushed and killed by Patterson's men.

Wearing a beard to keep himself unrecognized, Missouri watched the trial from the gallery.

In a surprise move, the defense called Mrs. Wilt to the stand. Although reluctant to testify, Marlena corroborated the testimony of an earlier witness that Wilt had set up the ambush himself to get both his enemies, Missouri and Patterson, out of the way by playing them off against one another. After that, court sentiment turned against Colonel Wilt. Old Patterson was exonerated.

His evil empire in disarray, Colonel Wilt made one last bid for power. He tricked the idealistic young marshall into drawing on Black Pete—Wilt was a genius at manipulating false evidence—and Pete, who was the best pure shooter in the territory, did the expected. With the marshall out of the way, Wilt sensed he could do pretty much what he wanted. His next move was to send a platoon of hired guns to cut off Paterson's water supply and torch his farm. The destruction of the farm was intended, in Wilt's scheme, as a provocation to force Patterson into reaching for his gun. Once Patterson had a gun in his hand, Wilt's minions could shoot the old farmer down like a dog under the guise of self-defense.

The only one who could put a stop to Wilt's unbridled ambition was Missouri. Using the night as cover, Missouri bush-wacked Wilt's hired guns at the pass, picking them off one by one, using of necessity his secondary hand, which was his right. The few survivors, led by Black Pete, retreated in desperation.

Meanwhile, Colonel Wilt, having already gone too far, went one step further. All restraint gone, he blew up the stagecoach carrying his wife, Marlena, and four innocent bystanders who were travelling east. The colonel, who had started out in life as a preacher, had let desperation and greed drive him into the abyss of his own private hell.

Conniving his way into Patterson's house, Wilt shot the old man in the back with a shotgun and was about to finish him off when Missouri appeared. Beating the arrogant Wilt to the draw in a fair fight, Missouri ended the robber baron's reign of terror with a single shot. For some reason now forgotten, a birthmark perhaps, a look around the eyes, the dying farmer recognized that Missouri was his long lost son, and there was a brief reconciliation between the two men, Patterson breathing his last breath in the gunfighter's arms, though not before telling Missouri that he and Wilt were the last remnants of a dying breed, prophesying that a new day was dawning in the west and that a time would come in Missouri's lifetime in which law would replace anarchy, and civilization the violent romance of the frontier.

The old west was not dead yet as it turned out. Learning that his friend, Missouri, was the enemy he had been looking for all his life, Black Pete challenged the retired gunfighter, who was about to leave town. Sick to death of killing, Missouri at first declined the challenge, but when he realized there was no avoiding the inevitable, a face-off was agreed to on the spot, and the two men circled each other, waiting for someone to make the first fatal move.

Before a gun was drawn or a shot fired, Tondelaya, the Indian Princess, arrived with conclusive evidence that Missouri was Pete's real father and just as father and son were being reunited, the former marshall's unstable older brother, who had been watching the shoot-out, shot Black Pete in the back, killing him instantly.

In later years, Missouri sublimated his loss by becoming the major distributor of firearms in his part of the west. He married Tondelaya, raised a family, ran for congress and then governor of the state, had even been talked about as a presidential possibility, when retroactive trauma broke him down twenty years after the traumatic event. The seedy coot had been drawing on imaginary gunfighters at the Bent Mind Retreat ever since.

If his story was true, Missouri would have been a hundred and ten years old at the time of its telling. His arrant implausibility engendered suspicion.

nineteen

What was beginning to concern me was not so much solving this case, uncovering the renegade agent, which I saw as doable, but the getting out of the asylum and on with my life after the case was solved. Whatever they say, the anointed experts on the subject, I happen to know that madness is as contagious as any biological infection.

The next inmate who opened himself up to me was a vaguely familiar aging juvenile who said his name was Archie Andrews. If I was skeptical, I nevertheless kept a straight face as I listened to the story of how he ended up at the Bent Mind Retreat. Things had been going swimmingly for Andrews. He had been appointed Secretary of Education by the Reagan administration and had just received an invitation from Clandestine High, his alma mater of twenty-five years before, to be the guest speaker at graduation.

His beautiful anorexic wife, Veronica, had taken leave from a rehab clinic in Minnesota for the occasion of Archie's speech and seemed distracted and edgy on the drive over in their government-issue limousine. Archie, on the other hand, was focused on making the speech of his life, was looking forward to a triumphant return.

There was an overflow crowd to see him perform, and inspired by the cheering and applause (some of it initiated by paid crowd-warmers), he put away his script, which was written for him by a team of experts, and spoke to his audience from the heart. He concluded his advice to the new graduates by saying, "It's all out there for the taking—we need only to reach out our hands aggressively and grab." With that, he held up his arms in a gesture of triumph and received a standing ovation, except for the malcontents in the crowd who stamped their feet and made hissing sounds.

Veronica, who had been dozing on the platform, woke in a sudden panic and fell from her chair. One drink for Veronica was like five for anyone else.

An old flame, Betty, the leader of a small radical feminist clique, had been arrested, Archie learned later that day—her absence had been conspicuous—for picketing the ceremony.

While Veronica was sleeping it off in their hotel room, Archie put up bail for Betty, and they went off together to renew old times at the local malt shop, which had relocated to the mall and updated its ambience. There was an immediate chemistry between them, an exchange of burning lookaway glances. Betty reached under the table and put her hand on his thigh, and Archie confided that in the early hours of the morning, unable to return to sleep, he often wondered what it would have been like to have Betty at his side. Moreover, it had been his secret aspiration as a teen to marry both Betty and Veronica and become a Mormon. "You haven't changed a bit, Archie," Betty said to him with exasperated affection. After that they got into Betty's car and drove to a motel on the edge of town.

Meanwhile, an old adversary named Reggie, who was a power broker and local pol living on the tattered edge of the law, was concerned that Archie had been sent by the government to expose his low level corruption. To forestall that possibility, Reggie had set up an outrageous plan to destroy Archie's credibility.

This was the way it happened. Veronica was in her hotel room, putting on her face while sipping booze from a flask, when there was some serious banging on her door. Before she could attend to it, a trio of narcotic agents burst in and started riffling through her personal things. Thinking the intruders were thieves, which was an honest mistake, Veronica got out the gun Archie had given her to protect herself and told the agents to freeze. She couldn't cover all three at once, and eventually they disarmed her and put her in cuffs. When quantities of cocaine and amphetamines were discovered (some of which were her own and some planted)—Veronica had been trying to cut down—she was arrested for drug possession, resisting arrest and solicitation.

At the same time, Archie and Betty, both wearing dark glasses, were photographed leaving the Bide Awhile Motel together. Archie ran after the photographer, tackled him in the street, and took the film out of his camera, but a crowd of people were watching, two of whom were reporters for the local paper and one a stringer for a wire service. In a matter of hours, Archie and Veronica's disgrace was broadcast everywhere, had become international news.

As they were packing their suitcases, looking to get out of town with the least possible notoriety, they tried to puzzle out what had happened to them.

"There's only one person mean enough to have done this," said Archie. "This frame-up's got our old friend Reggie's signature all over it."

A plan was hatched between them to pay Reggie back.

Wearing a sexually enticing pants suit, Veronica visited Reggie at his office at the Clandestine Golf and Gun Club and reminded him of a time when she was sweet sixteen and he had taken her into the country club woods pretending it was a short cut to the malt shop. "Let's see if the woods are still in place," said Reggie, and Veronica, playing to his vanity, led him by the hand. When they were completely out of sight, she put her gun to his ear and exacted a signed confession from the lowlife.

Just as Reggie was about to turn over the signed confession, one of his stooges appeared and got the draw on Veronica, forcing her to give up her gun.

When Archie arrived on the scene, Veronica was composing a suicide note at Reggie's insistence, so he snuck up behind Reggie and his paid stooge, and pressed a banana in each of their backs, ordering them to throw away their guns, which they did. Veronica collected the guns, putting her own back in her purse, and reclaimed Reggie's signed confession. Reggie, who always thought himself superior to Archie, pleaded for mercy and cursed the fates.

Moments after they had tied Reggie to a tree with a gag in his mouth, and Veronica had gone off with the villain's signed confession, an old friend of Archie's named Jughead, who was now one of Reggie's minions, appeared eating a pizza slice and carrying a gun.

Archie and Jughead, once best friends, faced each other at gun point, a disconcerting reunion.

Eventually, the balance of power altered once again, and Archie was tied to the tree in Reggie's place. Archie warned the thugs that it was a federal offense to point guns at a cabinet official, but his argument fell on sneering laughter. As soon as Archie was neutralized, Reggie dispatched his two hirelings to intercept Veronica who was on route to the authorities with his confession in her purse. Seemingly trapped, the cagey Veronica provoked her pursuers into chasing her into a cul de sac, and the two confused oafs ended up shooting each other.

While that was going on, Betty, who had her own agenda, wandered into the picture in time to see Reggie poking his gun under Archie's chin. Professing vengeful feelings toward her former boyfriend, she offered to do Reggie's dirty work for him.

"This is what I was hoping would happen," said Reggie, handing over his gun to her, and Betty untied Archie and ordered him to kneel in front of her.

"Do it," said Reggie, who was still under the delusion that Betty, whom he had married and divorced in short order several years ago, was on his side.

Then Betty turned her gun in Reggie's direction and told him she was making a citizen's arrest. Under the guise of reaching for a cigarette, Reggie came up with another gun and wildly fired at Betty, creasing her left shoulder. In a reflex response, Betty, who had always been an excellent shot, fired back, taking Reggie out of the game.

The government could fix anything it had a mind to in those days, and some agents were flown in to make the carnage look like the outcome of some crime family vendetta or, failing that, the work of some local sickie.

Anyway, Archie took the wounded Betty to his limousine which was waiting for him, Veronica in the back seat, at the entrance to the Clandestine Golf and Gun Club, and the three of them, Archie in the middle like old times, drove back to Washington to get on with the business of America. "We kicked some ass, didn't we?" Archie said, and everyone agreed, including the chauffeur who would later betray Archie to his superiors.

Two months later, Archie, whose real name I discovered from one of the nurses was Peter Price, was removed from his post as fallout of a nasty domestic scandal, and two years after that he became a permanent resident of the Bent Mind Retreat.

twenty

I interviewed two of the others in the ward, but there really was no need to. I knew after the first hour with him that the pseudonymous Archie was the man we were looking for, which was what I told my "sister" Maribeau, who had been my only contact with the Committee during my incarceration. I was required to file a report and at her next regular visit, Maribeau slipped me the appropriate forms. Peter Price, I alleged, after losing his soul to Countess Maria Moussakka, had become a hollow man, willing to do or be whatever his controllers wanted of him (his becoming a comic book character as a form of cover was a fitting final step). At this point, the poor guy was no danger to anyone, which was what I told the Committee in my report. Whoever or whatever Peter had betrayed, he had to have been under orders from higher up.

After six long months in the madhouse, I had become a loose cannon myself, a marginal loony tune, and I insisted on the other inmates calling me Jughead. As a consequence, Archie (Peter) and I became best friends again.

Unfortunately, my superiors felt that the danger remained that Peter would one day remember who he really was, that he was like a delayed time bomb waiting to go off, and that it was always better to err on the side of death. What I didn't expect was that I would be the one chosen to arrange for my

118

friend's permanent vacation. When Maribeau, who had been flirting with me over the several month period of our sham relationship, told me what the bosses wanted me to do, I absolutely refused. "I would do the same thing in your shoes," she said, "but they'll kill you anyway, bro."

Despite repeated threats, I held to my position, and instead of killing me outright, the Committee sent me on a kamikaze mission behind the iron curtain to kidnap an East German scientist working with the Russians, a former Nazi who was a pioneer in biological warfare. It took almost a year to convince the Russians that I was what I pretended, and by that time the German scientist had been assassinated by some other clique.

The trouble with pretense was that you were always in danger of taking your own con seriously.

Oddly, the agent the Russians used to "turn" me, as it's called, was my contact at the Retreat, my fake sister Maribeau, with whom I had been playing pretend incest off and on. Maribeau, whom I had met years back on Primavera Island, where she assisted the brilliant Dr. Y and ultimately betrayed him, was a double or triple agent in her own right. Anyway, along with Maribeau, I was snatched by the KGB and taken to East Germany, where I spent another several months being tested for loyalty in various time-consuming ways. I had a half a dozen secrets to retail, five of which the Russians already had from other sources.

The Communists couldn't seem to make up their minds whether to trust me or not, seemed to go back and forth in that regard, and the longer it took for me to penetrate their biological warfare center, the more my own side began to lose trust. Maribeau, who was also my contact with the Americans, said the people in charge had begun to lose interest in my mission. Then, just days after I was cleared for work with the relevant classified Soviet materials, I got sick and was sent home.

When I returned from my protracted undercover tour of duty behind the iron curtain—this during the latter stages of the cold war—I found myself suffering from an odd and humiliating disorder. I was subject to sneezing fits, tended from time to time to lose all sense of equilibrium and stumble into walls and fall on my face. In the back rooms, I was known as "the spy who came home with a cold," a reference to a popular movie of a few years back. The doctors I consulted, government and private, all of whom were eager to operate on my nervous system, had no useful answers.

My superiors suspected that the strain of being a spy in a world in which there was no clear cut right or wrong had turned me into a hopeless drunk (or worse), and they sent me to a clinic in North Dakota for drying out and rehab. When my ailment didn't respond to therapy, I was given disability leave, which I spent with Miriam Hart, who was a research doctor and the widow of my lookalike half-brother, Marco, who disappeared two years before under mysterious circumstances while bringing pain-relieving drugs to civil war victims in Eastern Europe. Marco and I had been separated at birth, and I had seen him only three times in thirty years, the last time at his wedding where, while acting as best man, I fell under the spell of his bride, who at one time had been my high-school sweetheart.

It was Miriam Hart (I had known her as Sassy), a scientist with a passion for the unknown, who uncovered the true nature of my mysterious ailment. Renegade Soviet scientists, working secretly with a Japanese computer firm, had developed an undetectable virus which, while lingering in the bloodstream, created a condition of slurred speech and chronic imbalance, a condition that simulated the symptoms of drunkenness down to the last detail. It was Miriam's theory that I had been infected with that experimental virus while on duty behind the iron curtain.

Miriam effected a short-term cure—each treatment lasted between three and five hours—by blowing the specially treated smoke of her cigarette into the tip of mine. Since the treatment had to be repeated over shorter and shorter intervals as its effects weakened, it enforced an inadvertent intimacy. One intimacy led to another, and eventually, perhaps because of my resemblance to Marco, perhaps because we were both at loose ends, Miriam and I became lovers. The around-the-clock sex, with which I was never fully comfortable, also retarded the symptoms of the virus.

Our idyll was short-lived. It soon became clear to me that to save my life and redeem my career, I had to return behind the iron curtain and steal the anti-virus. Miriam wanted to go along, didn't want to lose me as she had lost Marco, and I did everything in my power to dissuade her for her own good. When I saw that arguments were of no avail, I changed her mind—it seemed the only thing left to do—with one perfectly thrown sucker punch. "For love," I wrote on the pad next to the telephone, and then I closed the door behind me, expecting never to see Sassy again, holding on to the wall to keep from falling on my face.

With the help of former comrades in the spying trade, I worked my way into the secret headquarters of the Renegade Soviet Biological Center, where I discovered that my brother Marco, very much alive, was in charge of operations. Marco had always been the idealistic one, and I was shocked and disillusioned to discover him doing his biological magic for the other side.

There was something burnt out in Marco, and it was sad to see, particularly so in that our resemblance was so astonishing I had difficulty telling us apart. He let the security guards take me prisoner with only a shrug of regret. While being held captive at gun point and mocked by my captors, I spoke passionately (for Marco's sake alone) on the virtues of freedom. "Without freedom, we would be no different from the other side," I said, "except that we have tasted freedom and so know what we have lost." My captors gagged me at some point, but I could tell I had moved Marco to a fleeting moment of reconsideration.

All this was happening at a time when the Communist empire was beginning to come apart, and during the night a pro-democratic splinter group invaded the Center. In the crunch, brotherly feeling took precedence over ideology, and Marco offered me the antidote to the falling-down virus in exchange for a promise not to tell anyone at home that he had become cynical and corrupt. We shook hands on the deal, which would be the last time we would ever press brotherly flesh.

When the fight started, the good people—those opposed to biological warfare on both sides of the curtain—teamed up against the fanatics, and we eviscerated the infrastructure of the Communist dictatorship. The good guys, most of us, escaped with our lives and the formulas, including samples, of some pretty nasty stuff. One of the brothers was killed in the melee and one survived. The thing was, virtually no one could tell us apart.

*

I came home from the wars as my brother, Marco, only to find that Miriam had fallen in love with another, and that other would never come back to her. I consoled her in her grief, but I was the wrong man (even though the right one), and eventually I gave up trying to clear up an impossibly complex misunderstanding of my own making and went on to something else.

twenty-one

It was on the flight to New York from San Francisco during an experience of turbulence that my memory opened like a flower, and I relived meeting and falling hopelessly in love with a woman on a flight from Paris to San Francisco (with a stopover in New York) some indefinable time back. Her name was Marisan, and she was half French and half Vietnamese and all beautiful. What had happened to her? I wondered. And then it struck me—it had been gone from memory all this time—that she was the one, it was Marisan, who had been waiting for me to return at the Paradise Hotel.

About an hour before our scheduled arrival at Kennedy, the pilot announced that our flight would have to detour to Baltimore because of a winter storm with gale force winds off the coast of New York. All three New York City area airports were temporarily closed.

Filled with a sense of urgency, I rented a Mercury Marquis at the Baltimore airport, which I lost control of on the slick highway about ten miles out, skidding into an embankment and totaling the car. That I was able to walk when I climbed out of the wreckage seemed sufficient reason to continue the trip. Since I was miles from public transportation, I decided to hitch the rest of the way and was lucky to catch a ride almost immediately from two semi-attractive women, which turned out to be a mixed blessing. In trouble with the law and short of cash, the women pressed me to assist them in the robbery of a convenience store. While the robbery was in progress—I was supposed to be waiting for them in the car— I convinced a passing trucker, who was on his way to Secaucus, New Jersey, to take me as far as he was going. I wished the women well, though I had no time (and not much inclination) to help them with their lawless binge.

Two rides later, in the early morning of the next day, I reached New York City, which was in the midst of a sleet storm with gale force winds. It took me what seemed an age—a life-time—to get through the Lincoln Tunnel, which had one lane closed because of flooding.

After a two-mile walk in a lashing storm—my injuries from the crash beginning to make themselves felt—I some-how found myself across the street from the Paradise Hotel. The icy rain had moved inside my clothes, and my hands were numb, but it no longer seemed to matter. I had arrived; I was all but there.

Crossing in short steps in the high winds, balance pre-carious, the street caked with sleet—a car coming from nowhere barrelling toward me—I lost my footing and fell, hit-ting my forehead on the curb as I threw myself forward to apparent safety.

I knew as I picked myself up after a few moments (an hour? a night?) of lost time that there was somewhere I had to be. Pulled in several directions at once, I found myself para-lyzed with confusion. When I looked up, the clouds were parting—the storm had lost its furor, the new day was making its way—and I saw, or imagined I saw, a heavenly marquee with my name in lights above the title. The title my name pre-ceded was *The Man Who Invented the World*. Hallucination or not, I took it as a message from a higher power. Hollywood was calling to me, the cultural center of America, the arena of my brightest hopes. A comeback to the glory days was indi-cated. If so, what was I doing, caked with ice and mud, standing in front of the Paradise Hotel, on the rump end of the conti-nental dream? I wandered in a daze for a few blocks, and then a cab found me, and I went to Kennedy Airport with a sense of having done exactly the same thing once, perhaps twice be-fore. On account of the weather, there were no flights leaving for Los Angeles for another five hours. My motor racing, I fell asleep in one of those molded plastic chairs as if it had imagined my body alone in the formula of its design, and dreamed of flying west to that indeterminate point where the earth ended and the days of heaven began.

part 3

twenty-two

The next several years—the decade of my forties—had been so event-filled that I had no time to dwell on the haunting feeling of inner loss that plagued me during the early hours of the morning when sleep left me for choicer opportunities. There was something missing from my life, a nagging absence, that made itself felt whenever I paused for self-consideration, but fortunately (or not), through an extended period of displaced ambition and occasional pleasure, I had more than my share of preoccupying distractions. The centerpiece of these distractions was a visit to the Star Planet, which is in an uncharted galaxy billions of miles away. There is life outside of earth, but for all its superior intelligence, it is petty and inhuman and so in the last analysis, terminally disappointing. In any event, the experience of being in another universe centered me, and I came back to the states a more poised and self-possessed man than when I left. I also had come into some serious money, so I used the cachet it brought me to return to Hollywood as a producer of independent films. I completed two features—the best known a film about the days of decadence leading up to the French Revolution called *The Last Musketeer*. I had a terrific picture in the works for my third film, a bittersweet comedy about a failed stand-up comic who has a second career in heaven, when the following incident changed the direction of my life once again. This was how it happened.

I got up from my table at the Russian Tea Room—I was having dinner with a young writer-director—to call Lola, a woman I had been married to twice but hadn't seen in years. I got up from my table to confirm arrangements for our liaison later that evening at the very moment some duplicitous international agent was being paged by the people hoping to trap him. Once I was mistaken for this ostensibly dangerous figure, a man as it were of a thousand faces, a man who might not even exist, my life was inescapably altered. I became a figure adrift in an irrational universe.

Two men with guns discreetly displayed approached me as I was getting into a phone booth and directed me outside into a black stretch limo. They identified me as a Mr. Philip Levy.

The more I insisted I was not this Mr. Levy, the more convinced they seemed to be that I was no one but. When I tried to leap out of the car door at a red light, they laughed at me for behaving like an amateur. "You are one funny guy, Mr. Levy," the shorter of my two captors said, doubled over with amusement.

I was taken to an elegant country estate belonging to the famous criminal lawyer, Wilfred Cog, defender of high-profile lost causes, where I was grilled by Mr. Cog himself, an over-civilized white-haired man with an English or vaguely German accent. "What is your assignment, Mr. Levy?" he asked repeatedly. I sensed that if my captors didn't get what they wanted, whatever that was, my life was not worth a plugged nickel or a hill of beans or the front page of yesterday's newspaper.

Still I told them nothing, had no state secrets to sell, playing the false role (while continuing to deny I was the man they sought) I had unwittingly inherited. After a while I pitched a few stories at my captors, which though credible in some ways—they were from my stock of movie treatments under development—didn't fully assimilate into their version of the real world. Amused by my stories, they nevertheless talked of drowning me in a bathtub or of pouring whiskey down my throat and taking me for a one-way ride to nowhere. If they were trying to scare me, it was the one thing they had done so far, in my regard, with some measure of success. "But what is your real story?" Mr. Cog insisted.

Their constant questioning had battered my resistance. Why not tell them the real story, I thought.

My life runs through the Paradise Hotel, was the way I started, but that's old news and it's personal stuff, though the personal and political are sometimes inseparable. After the loss of a loved one, I was drinking heavily and doing some private detection during my semi-sober hours, pretending to be a post-man as a form of cover while following this man, supposedly my client's husband (though she had given me the picture of her lover by mistake), and in the course of my pursuit, I rang the bell of a turn-of-the-century manor house set off from the road. A seductive, almost beautiful blonde opened the door— the kind of woman who had always spelled trouble for me—and invited me to come in for a cool glass of lemonade. I declined her offer—I knew if I went inside I would get in-volved in something way over my head. I would fall in love with the woman, become her lover, conspire with her to re-move the obstacle in the path of our happiness, which would mean killing her husband. Distracted by the inevitable sce-nario playing through my mind, I was slow to withdraw, observing the woman fish through her purse and a small pis-tol flash in her hand. "Wait a minute," I started to say, but she fired at me point blank, a secretive smile on her face, and I fell backward from the impact of the shot, my mouth agape in surprise, my hands out in front of me fending off the fatal bullet as if it hadn't already come and gone.

I woke on a soupy bed in a glitzy sleazebag hotel room, the room littered with empty fifths of vodka, a woman I could swear I didn't know asleep with her head imbedded in my shoulder, a wedding ring on her third finger left hand.

When I lifted her head to retrieve my shoulder, the woman, who had been snoring, woke up without opening her eyes to complain about being abused in her sleep.

"Do we know each other?" I asked her. She had to pull her eyes open to squint at me. "My name will come to me in a minute,"she said. "Don't go away."

Eventually the cobwebs cleared, and we introduced our-selves by whatever name we each happened to be using at the moment. She was Marie Montevanni, which was the name on her driver's license. I had met her in Las Vegas apparently, where she had come to marry her childhood sweetheart. Somehow the bozo got into a private high-stakes card game with me and a few others and lost not only his shirt but his bride-to-be. Having won her less than an hour before her wedding, I was obliged, I supposed, to marry her, which I did to no one's apparent satisfaction.

This hellhole hotel room with brocaded illustrations from the karma sutra on red-velvet walls, where we found ourselves in drunken torpor, was our inadvertent honeymoon arena. I offered to take her back to her fiance, but she said no, she was a married woman now and would make the best of her situation. Besides, she said, blowing her nose and blinking back tears, she was not the kind to marry a man who would put her up as collateral in a poker game.

So we stayed together a few more days, moving into the Culture Shock suite of the same hotel, and did all the things honeymooners do except that we were drunk most of the time we were doing them. Then her boyfriend showed up, grim and apologetic and angry, all by turns, asking for another chance.

When she refused to go with him, the fiance, Wyn Salem, lifted Marie in his arms and carried her off, her protests made with minimal conviction. As she was my wife, even though I had no recollection of marrying her, I pursued the runaway couple in a stolen Cadillac, trailed them into the wastelands of New Mexico.

Something happened to me in New Mexico, something more important than recovering a wife I barely knew, and after what happened my priorities shifted radically, and I found my life moving in a new direction. It all started with a dream, a remarkable dream which has stayed with me, a dream so lifelike it persuaded me of its claim to some higher truth. The dream began with Marie shaking me from sleep and repeating three times that I had visitors waiting for me in the desert behind the house. "I hope you know them, Max," she said, "because I sure as hell don't."

There was something like a space vehicle in the backyard with an aura of light around it so dazzling that it was impossible to make out any of its details. I was taken aboard this UFO in an unthreatening way by a group of shadowy extraterrestrials and invited to lie down on a narrow black table. One of the creatures wearing a mask of a human face that resembled an obscure figure from the 70s rock scene examined me in great detail, using bizarre medical utensils that were feathery to the touch. The last thing I remember before falling asleep was my penis being prodded and an almost human voice saying, "Peace be with you, brother."

I woke up in the driver's seat of my pale-pink Cadillac in a cold sweat, Marie, whom I hadn't seen outside of a few cameo dream apparances in almost two weeks, seated next to me, reading the magazine, *Vanity Fair*. I was occupied with my dream and insisted on telling it to her, though it was clear she had little or no interest in hearing me out. At one point, she interrupted my story with an exasperated sigh. "I've heard that story before," she said. "Wyn had the same crazy dream. That's all he talked about, day and night; I couldn't stand to be in the same room with him after a while."

I was a skeptical humanist by inclination, not readily seduced by the unlikely, until I noticed a narrow, barely perceptible scar on my thigh where one of the alien implements had apparently made a small incision. It was time to get some answers, and I started up the Cadillac, and we drove through the night to the National Bureau of Inexplicable Phenomena, which was exactly a hundred miles from our Los Alamos motel.

"This isn't exactly what I want to do with my life," Marie said as we sped along the naked highway. "I'm only going along because you're my husband."

The first three bureaucrats I told my story to treated me like a potentially dangerous lunatic, and I had the sense, hearing my own words come back to me in a kind of echo, of how truly unbelievable my story must have sounded. Then, wandering the corridors of the windowless building looking for Marie, I overheard a long-haired type with a pony tail, telling a heavy-set man wearing thick-lensed glasses virtually the same story of abduction and examination I had been telling. "Wait a minute," I said. "That's my story."

The listener, who introduced himself as Dr. Pratt, turned to me and said, "Not only do I believe you boys believe you're telling the truth, I believe that what you describe as having happened to you did in fact happen." That was a relief to hear, but there was something odd about the doctor, something not quite real. He said if we were interested in making contact with other folks who've had similar experiences, there would be a meeting in the basement for the "chosen" in approximately twenty minutes.

Right after that we ran into Wyn Salem, who said he no longer blamed me for stealing his wife. His experience with the extraterrestrials had made him a wiser and gentler man. I noticed then that he had a war wound, which caused him to drag his left leg. It was then I realized that my accidental wife was the same Marie whose father I worked for in Boston years back, the one who had a thing for men with disabling handicaps.

Marie said she could no longer choose between us, so she was going off to the Encounter Lounge to drown her sorrows.

There was a crowd of people in Pratt's basement when Salem and I got there, the room abuzz with slightly varied versions of the same story. Pratt walked up to the front of the room and introduced himself. "My name is Dr. William F. Pratt, and I'm here to tell you that you have not been hallucinating; you folks are no more crazy than I am." There was some applause and a few shouts of "you can say that again." Holding up his hands to silence the excited crowd, Pratt continued. "All of us here share a unique experience for which we've been mocked and reviled," he said. "People, it's time to put the mocking and reviling to rest. Justification Day is at hand."

Pratt went on to tell us that he had received word through private intergalactic channels that our visitors from another universe had agreed to make a public appearance at a site to be announced—probably Disney World—eight days from today to prove to the mockers and revilers that we were not loony tunes but people with special qualities. There was a spy among us, a man dressed in black who slipped out before Pratt's speech was over. I decided to follow him and see what was afoot. The spy, who had written down Pratt's words on the back of an envelope, resembled my troubled friend, Peter Price.

Peter, who had been in and out of government service before breaking down and taking on the identity of a comic book character, went directly to Colonel Septic's office in another part of the building and reported Pratt's claim that the aliens had agreed to make a public appearance as a way of making common cause with their supporters. "These people who don't exist cannot be allowed to appear," Septic, who was the Commander-in-Chief of Inexplicable Phenomena, said to the man who may or may not have been my old friend. "If these aliens show themselves, our credibility as a space agency will be totally destroyed. We've always denied the existence of UFOs because it is not information the general public is equipped to handle. For the sake of our country's mental health, this unauthorized visitation must be nipped in the bud." After that, in stentorian whispers, a counterplot, of which I was able to get only a few details, was set in motion.

Before I could return to the basement and inform Dr. Pratt of Colonel Septic's plot against him, my presence was discovered, and I was taken into custody by Septic's people and locked in a padded cell with the drunken Marie who had also been captured eavesdropping. By the time we escaped with the help of a guard who had had a personal visitation from the aliens, we had thirty-six hours to get to Disney World to warn Dr. Pratt.

The airports and railroad stations were closely guarded by Septic's men, so we had to make the trip by personal vehicle, which we did, stopping only to go to the bathroom, trade in the car to avoid pursuers, and pick up fuel for ourselves and our transportation. We took turns sleeping, and it was not always the one not driving who slept.

Since the area around Disney World was barricaded for security reasons, we had to jettison the car and make our way through the Everglades on foot, arriving at Disney World in a state of exhilarated exhaustion barely three minutes before countdown.

Pratt was on a stage when we arrived, dressed in one of those white guru gowns, and I had to push my way through security to reach him. He was standing in front of a giant sign with the inscription, WELCOME EXTRATERRESTRIALS!!! PLEASE CHECK IN ON ARRIVAL AT DESK SEVEN.

It was hard to get his attention among all the fanfare— two marching bands spelling out WE LOVE YOU, ET'S, the Mouseqeteers doing an old Elvis Presley song, "Hound Dog," at ear-splitting pitch on the loud-speaker system; Mickey, Donald, Minnie and Goofy dancing and goofing around—but

Pratt recognized me and shook my hand warmly, saying he was glad I could make it. When I told him about Septic's plot to destroy the aliens, he took me inside a large tent, which had a number of TV monitors going. One of them showed Septic and a small army of followers on some camouflaged mountaintop with two manned missile launchers, apparently waiting for the spaceship to enter their line of fire.

Pratt's unconcern concerned me, and I asked if there was anything I could do to help, which only made him smile in his odd affectless way. "They have their thing to do," he said, "and we have ours."

The countdown was starting over the loudspeaker ...100...99...98......75...74...73....

At the count of 20, a glowing saucer much like the one in my dream flashed by above us. On the TV monitor, Colonel Septic was giving the signal to fire.

A small girl in our crowd stage-whispered to her mother, "They're here."

I watched the TV monitor in horror as the missile from Septic's mountain base made contact with the saucer, disintegrating it as if it were a minor obstruction in a video game. The crowd let out a mournful cry that I would not soon forget.

"Not to worry," Pratt said over the loudspeaker, pleading with the disheartened crowd of believers for a moment of silence. "The unidentified flying object you saw shot out of the sky was a decoy in the form of a hologram."

Wyn Salem, among others, was standing next to Pratt on the great stage, and I overheard Salem ask why Pratt's people had chosen the Elvis Presley song, "Hound Dog," to honor the aliens' visit.

"Because," said Pratt, "and this is not to be repeated outside this immediate circle, he was one of them, which is to say one of us. They sent him to us from a world on the other side of the sky when he was only an infant, as a sign of their intended friendship. He was their king too." Pratt reached down under his chin and peeled back the skin-tight mask covering his real face, which was the face of the older, bloated Elvis. The surprising appearance, amidst all the other surprises, evoked a sustained shriek from the crowd.

There was another flash of light and a spaceship appeared in the parking lot, a huge door sliding open to form a ramp.

A theatrical spotlight waited for the emergence of the aliens, and the collective expectation of the crowd was like an electrical charge. The first to emerge was John Lennon, followed by Bobby Kennedy, Judy Garland, Lee Harvey Oswald, Andy Warhol, and Jimmy Hendrix. Marilyn Monroe came next, and her name passed through the hushed crowd like a blessing. Pratt explained over the loudspeaker system that these stars had been aliens first and had been loaned to earth in a perceived time of need as a gesture of divine love from his celebrity planet. "We've come back for only a brief interlude this time," he said, "but we will come back again and again if you continue to love and remember us."

Pratt then said that five of us would be permitted to visit the Star Planet, the names to be drawn out of a hat. Among the five chosen was Wyn Salem—his was the only name that I recognized—the crowd cheering as three men and two women marched into the spotlight to board the saucer. "Don't go," Marie called to Salem, whose limp seemed to have exacerbated. "I love you, Wyn."

"I love you too, Marie," Wyn said, breaking ranks and limping toward her as she ran toward him. Everything stood frozen in time, waiting for them to meet and embrace.

It was then that Wyn asked me to take his place, which I had done in a sense once before, and, accepting the loss of Marie, I boarded the saucer with the others, the door sliding shut behind me like an extended hush.

There was no time to reconsider. In the next moment we were spaceborne, speeding at some heartbreaking rate to our remote destination in the universe.

twenty-three

The Star Planet, where I was to spend my next five years, was a semi-replica of Earth, except that its cities were elaborate stage sets, and virtually nothing existed beyond its impressive facade. It was a culture enormously advanced in certain ways—its technology at the level of our most exotic science-fiction fantasies—but at the same time the general populace was disconcertingly naive and credulous. All rumors and gossip were accepted as unshakeable truths. Disbelievers (and discontents) were considered unstarlike and kept out of the public eye.

No one seemed to do much on SP, celebrity its own vocation, and the average citizen tended to watch videos on huge screen wraparound home televisions for most of the day. Basic necessities were provided by the government, making work a marginal option chosen, according to official figures, by less than twenty percent of the population.

The five of us from earth were treated as celebrities for about a year or so after our arrival—we did a public appearance tour across the planet and gave interviews (in which we were wildly misquoted) to the gossip sheets they called newspapers—and then we were forgotten.

I took no pleasure in being idle, and I set up shop as a private investigator, while waiting for the next saucer back to

Earth. There was not much business since the only crimes on the Star Planet had to do with psychosis (abberation, as they called it) and not need. Anything and everything the celebrity citizenry wanted was available to them. It was a society in which happiness was perceived not only as the highest good, but as the only viable option.

When I arrived, most of the gossip concerned a warlike planet in the galaxy, the Insidious Empire, which had been threatening to invade SP over a series of ever-changing trumped-up issues. According to the analysis in the local tabloids, the IE was an expansionist planet seeking domination of the galaxy for murky pernicious reasons. In any event, someone from the government, an official spokescelebrity, came to see me, asking unofficially if I would lead an exploratory expedition into an outpost of the Insidious Empire, the government desiring insider information on the latest technology of this perceived potential enemy. I said I would need some time to think about it, and then something else came my way—an intriguing new case—that knocked the other consideration clear out of mind.

A gray-haired woman of uncertain age (resembling Anne Bancroft) came to see me in my new office, which simulated the tackiness of the dives I used to work out of in the states, with an extraordinary story. Her only son, Raymond, who had always been as good a boy as a mother could want, she said, might have gotten himself into a bad situation. She had been both mother and father to poor Raymond, never letting the boy out of her sight, never letting the boy stray from the appropriate path. One day, however, she left Raymond to do some shopping and came home to find him with some strange woman in his room and the door, which was always to be kept ajar, firmly shut. When she heard giggling behind the closed door, she called out to Raymond to warn him of her imminent appearance. As she opened Raymond's door, she heard the sound of breaking glass and noticed Raymond lying face down on his bed. The slut, as Mrs. Shaw referred to her, in her haste to leave, had thrown herself through the window. Mrs. Shaw tried to comfort "the poor boy," but he was inconsolable.

She thought that was the end of it, but two years later another slut was found beheaded in an unoccupied apartment across the street, and a photo of Raymond's mother was found tacked to the wall above the corpse, implying some kind of unwholesome connection. Raymond was still living at home then, but shortly after this incident he moved out without leaving a forwarding address.

Raymond's mother wanted me to find the boy, who was now in his early thirties, and clear his name. No matter how incriminating the situation appeared, she said, she believed in the boy's basic goodness. It was a recent episode, the third of its kind, that had brought the woman to seek my help. "Someone is going to great lengths to prove Raymond's bad," she said.

Though her story had its questionable aspects, I agreed to take the case, warning her that the solution might topple her preconceptions. She laughed and said she had not a single doubt in her mind as to Raymond's innocence, giving me a semi-recent photo of her son, a profile shot mostly in shadow.

Since there was no crime, or no acknowledged crime on the Star Planet, the central police station was only open three days a week. On the first available day, I went to see the Chief, a burly, familiar-looking black man (everyone on the planet looked like some Earth movie star or other) named Jim E. Jones (called Jonesy), and I asked him what he knew about the recent rash of beheadings. "You think we need some know-it-all Earthling to teach us our business here," he said, roaring with laughter at his goodnatured jibe. "Case solved. Perpetrator in police custody."

One of his officers, a newcomer to the force, had picked up a former mental patient wandering about at the scene of the crime and had made the collar.

I showed him the out-of-focus picture I had of Raymond and asked if this was the man.

He studied the picture for a moment before acknowledging the possibility. "That's the man who made the arrest," he said. "That's our new officer, Raymond Shaw."

I asked him what he knew about Shaw and he laughed at me in his good-natured mocking way and said, "What does anyone know about anyone?" Then he said the detective work of Earthlings always amused him and he was particularly looking forward to the results of my inspired meddlesome bumbling.

It took me a week more of meddling and the witnessing of a brutal murder to discover that Mrs. Shaw's judgment of her son's innocence was technically correct. Raymond appeared to be the killer, though it was another one of those untrustworthy illusions the Star Planet was famous for. The solution came to me in a dream. Having killed her beloved son in an accident, Mrs. Shaw had incorporated his identity as a means of keeping Raymond alive. It was the Raymond side of the personality that did the killing, while the mother side covered up for the disfunctional son she had loved not wisely but too well.

When I went to see Jonesy and laid out my solution—I also had a photo of the Raymond mask the mother wore when she became Raymond—he said it was not only more amusing than he anticipated, it also sounded extremely reasonable. Nevertheless, he put me in jail for the night (for my own safety, he said), in a stage-set cell that only had walls on two sides. He let me go the next day with the warning that if I interfered in police business again I would lose my star status and be deported as an undesirable alien. Since the case had already been solved—didn't he have a perpetrator behind bars?—my solution was redundant. It struck me that no matter where you go, the obvious is always out there waiting to surprise you.

About a month later, the events I just described appeared on television as the featured Movie of the Week. I caught it as a rerun one sleepless night and had to look away from the screen in embarrassment whenever I appeared. The movie had a coda where the detective appeals to Jonesy one last time to reconsider and Jonesy, arm around his shoulders, leads him into the next room where we hear this high-pitched laugh. Nothing is revealed.

The words, THE END, appear on the blackened screen.

The next two cases that came my way were mirror images of ones I had handled back on earth, and I could sense a pattern beginning to emerge. One concerned a woman who woke every other morning with an unfamiliar dead man in bed next to her, and the other was brought to me by a sexy older woman who wanted me to help her dispose of a disagreeable husband half her age. And then a case offered itself concerning a serial killer who got his kicks throwing people out of high-story windows. I rejected all of these cases on the same grounds: I did not want to spend my life, even in a faraway place, rehashing old triumphs.

*

Wilfred Cog was getting impatient with me. "Where is this all leading?" he asked. "When do we get to the details of your mission?"

"That comes next," I said.

twenty-four

I was at loose ends when the detection business staled, and I agreed under pressure from the authorities to head a fact-finding expedition to a remote outpost off the westernmost coast of the Insidious Empire, a more compelling option than hanging out on the Star Planet wearing the required happy smile until my mouth turned to rictus. Anyway, my spokescelebrity contact had given me his written promise that as soon I returned from a place called Lunatha with the information they sought, they would run an unscheduled space shuttle to take me back to Earth. I had no idea when I accepted their devious offer that the odds on the expedition's safe return were 8 to 1 against.

They outfitted me with an experienced crew of space travelers, all of whom were in the twilight of their celebrity, all of whom, like myself, were seeking a shot at redemption.

The mission was classified Double Top Secret. Our instructions, which were kept in a sealed envelope (inside another sealed envelope) in a locked metal box, were not to be opened until we landed successfully on the dark side of Lunatha.

Before we made it to Lunatha, we got blindsided by some random space garbage, making it necessary to crash land on the Isle of Dreams—the only port in a storm between Star

143

Planet and Insidious Empire—to repair the neural damage. We thought a two-day layover would suffice to get us space-worthy again, but we ended up spending almost two weeks on the pernicious island before getting away, some of us, with our lives.

There was something in the gravitational pull of the tides surrounding I.O.D that made its inhabitants' dream-life so disconcertingly real and dangerous. Dream figures moved in and out of the waking world on this loathsome island, sometimes causing terror and even death, refusing to limit themselves to the traditional boundaries of sleep. For that reason, I ordered the crew to stay on board while the damage to the ship's nervous system was being repaired. The mistake I made was not obeying my own directives.

We had picked up on our Viewfinder screen the indication that some semi-human creature (with a lizard-like face) was pursuing an extremely pretty teenaged girl in the boiler room of the local high-school, trying to decapitate her with a samurai sword. Someone ought to look into this, I thought, and leaving the ancient android, Gilgamesh, in charge, I went off in a space boat, which was the size of one of those three-wheeled buggies cops in the states use to give out parking tickets, to check out the situation.

When I arrived on the scene, Lizard Face, as I thought of him, had been charred to ashes and the girl, whose name I later learned was Dottie Gale, was huddled in a corner, flame thrower at her feet, trembling with fright. "Who or what was he?" I asked her.

"That's my dream half-brother, Lenny," she said. "Whenever I close my eyes, he's there, trying to do something unspeakable to me."

Clearly he was dead and could do her no more harm, but she insisted, incredible as it sounded, that she had killed him twice before. Nevertheless, as a creature of her dreams, he had the power to return whenever she fell asleep. Then she told me the following story.

Two years back, Lenny had been a recurring figure in her nightmares when suddenly he began to appear at school and at sex parties she went to with her friends, usually wearing a hockey mask and carrying a chain saw. When she told the authorities about him, no one (not even her mother and her mother's boyfriend) took her seriously. What they did was take her to a psychiatrist who seemed to think she had imagined Lenny because she was jealous of her baby brother. The thing Lenny liked least, it turned out, was to be the subject of disbelief. In a murderous rampage, he killed Dottie's mother, boyfriend, and baby brother, leaving his bloody sword in Dottie's bed as evidence against her. Fortunately for Dottie, her psychiatrist, a Dr. Waters, was one of the few others for whom Lenny had reality, and between them (her boyfriend Ray also participating), they were able to freeze the nasty creature in a block of ice.

A year and half passed, and Dottie, living with a new family in a different suburb on the island, began to dream of Lenny again. Shortly after the dreams recurred, the creature claiming to be her half-brother reappeared, even uglier this time than before, and the old horrors recapitulated. Fortunately she remembered that Lenny was susceptible to fire, and, as I had witnessed, she had incinerated him to ashes with an army surplus flame thrower someone had carelessly left lying around in the high-school boiler room, bringing Lenny's unspeakable career to its second apparent end. Nevertheless, the child—she could have been no more than fourteen—remained in a state of terror, convinced that unless she got off the Isle of Dreams she would be hounded by the monstrous dream creature forever.

I told her there was no way I could take her with us, that we were on a double top-secret dangerous mission, but she seemed so damaged by her encounter with the abominable Lizard Face, I ended up bringing her back to the ship, so that our resident doctor could examine her.

There were no complaints from the crew, though Marilyn, the only other woman aboard, rolled her eyes a bit when I carried Dottie aboard, the girl's arms wrapped around my neck.

Doctor Gillespie talked to me about Dottie's condition. "There's more here than meets the eye, Max," he said. "As long as the little gal continues to believe that Lenny exists, she'll never be free of him."

"But he does exist," I said, "or did."

For some reason, our mechanic was having trouble completing repairs and the crew began to believe that someone or something was sabotaging his efforts, which was another source of discord.

*

That night I had a disturbing dream in which Dottie figured in a surprising way.

I was watching Dr. Gillespie examine the girl through a glass partition. He had a long narrow flashlight which he was using to look down her throat, the girl seemingly asleep, though periodically shaken by minor spasms. A clawed reptilian hand suddenly sprung from the girl's mouth and grasped the astonished doctor's wrist. Momentarily, the flashlight and then the doctor's arm disappeared down the girl's gullet which seemed to enlarge to accommodate its prey. The doctor struggled, but whatever was yanking his arm was too powerful for him to resist, and before I could come to his rescue—his door was locked, the surrounding glass unbreakable—the arm was torn from its socket as it was dragged down the girl's throat. The sight staggered me, but I kept by turns pushing and pulling at the door, trying to decode its resistance. I woke in a sweat, my heart beating frantically, just as the door seemed to give way.

When I got to the doctor's quarters, neither Dottie nor Dr. Gillespie were available, and I assumed they were at mess with the others.

An hour later when I brought the crew together for a briefing, the doctor was not among them, which concerned me, and I asked in an offhanded manner, not wanting to alarm the others, if anyone knew where Gillespie had gone. Either no one had seen him or no one was willing to admit to having seen him. Dottie also was among the missing.

I sent out a search committee of two to find our missing doctor and his patient, and when they didn't return I sent out a second team of searchers. And then a third. When several hours passed and none of the missing had returned, I began to wonder if my dream of the previous night hadn't touched on something real.

Dottie was the first one to reappear. She announced to all of us that her dream brother, Lenny, had gotten aboard ship (even though all entrances to our vehicle, Space Tramp, had been sealed off) and had kidnapped the doctor.

"What does he want?" I asked Dottie.

"He wants everything," she said. "He'll stop at nothing."

"Where have you been all this time, little girl?" Marilyn asked in a suspicious voice. The others echoed her concern.

Dottie said she had been hiding, afraid for her life, moving from one compartment to another.

"I think you're our problem," Marilyn said, and then Dottie did this odd thing, started talking to Marilyn as if Marilyn were Lenny, as if Lenny had taken over Marilyn, which she said was one of his powers. The argument got nastier as charges and countercharges were leveled between them.

The argument divided the crew, some supporting Marilyn's contentions, some Dottie's.

Solo Pilgrim suggested that we quarantine the both of them until a test could be devised to determine which one was telling the truth.

This suggestion suited everyone but Marilyn, who said, "How do we know anyone is telling the truth?"

Then Dottie said, "The fair thing to do would be to quarantine everyone until the test is given, since Lenny could be any of us or all of us."

The logistics of quarantining everyone seemed prohibitively difficult, so I said, "Why don't we just stay together and keep an eye on each other." The dispute continued for another hour, the distrust among us intensifying.

We took turns standing watch that night, all of us in the Video Library, which was our largest common room. When I completed my watch, I fell asleep almost immediately and had another compelling, life-like dream.

The dream was set in the officers' mess. We were eating egg salad sandwiches—some of us with our heads on the table taking a nap—when Lenny, wearing Dr. Gillespie's clothes, came sneering into the room. Chuck Heston stepped in front of him, and the monster, using one razorlike finger, sliced our elder statesman virtually in half. We all recoiled at the gruesome sight, frightened for our own survival. "Go away, Lenny," Dottie said to him. "No one here believes in you." And momentarily Lenny vanished, the crew applauding as if Dottie had performed a magic trick.

When I woke, Chuck Heston was among the missing, the room awash in blood (or red paint), the Video screen flashing on and off like a neon light.

147

Among the four survivors beside myself were Gilgamesh, the Pilgrim brothers (Solo and Skye) and Dottie Gale. There were no corpses in the room; the others had simply vanished.

As commander of the expedition, I ordered our immediate departure, instructing our highly evolved computer (the most advanced of the Hank V series) to take us without further delay to our assigned destination. In moments our ship, though still partially disabled, took off in an explosion of flames for Lunatha.

Distrust among us was at a fever pitch, most of it centered on Dottie, whose arrival had, at the very least, circumstantial connection to our recurrent problems. There was some sentiment for leaving her behind on the Isle of Dreams. Instead, as a form of compromise, we had Dottie locked in the doctor's cabin, injected with caffein to keep her awake and bound (like a butterfly in a cocoon) by a truss of silk threads. The rest of us, armed with flame throwers against Lenny's reappearance, took sanctuary in our own quarters while the Space Tramp, navigated by Hank V, headed toward what we mistakenly thought was the dark side of Lunatha.

I didn't dare sleep, fought myself to stay awake, until we landed safely at our destination.

twenty-five

Lenny and Dottie, as it turned out, were really two opposing aspects of the same personality—a version of the Jeckyl and Hyde duality—and it was only after Dottie was killed in a bizarre twist of fate that we were rid of the monstrous Lenny. Although the evidence was apparent all along, it took me awhile to discover that Lenny did not exist without Dottie. It was that discovery that saved my life and set me up for the betrayal waiting for me when we reached our destination.

When the Space Tramp landed on what I thought was Lunatha, a remote outpost of the Insidious Empire, I was the only non-android still alive. Although I didn't see how the mission might be completed without the others, I nevertheless opened the sealed instructions governing this double top secret assignment.

Before I get to the particulars of my orders—my hidden assignment—which were not at all what I expected, I think I'd better backtrack a bit and tell you how I discovered that Dottie and Lizard Face were reverse sides of the same coin. During the night, while the others were asleep, I went to the cabin where Dottie was imprisoned to see if there was anything I could do to ease her burden. To my surprise, she was

149

gone, and in her place, bound and gagged, was the ship's doctor, who had been missing since yesterday and was generally thought to be dead.

I released the doctor and asked for an explanation. As the doctor collected his thoughts, a rumble seemed to come up from his throat, a thunderous rumble that got louder and louder as it reached his lips. "Insidious Empire," he moaned, repeating the name as if he hadn't made himself clear the first time, and then his stomach swelled and split open, Lenny emerging in full reptilian glory. Fortunately, I had the flame thrower with me, strapped to my back. I escaped this confrontation with a few slash wounds on my arms and legs, deceived in the belief that I had destroyed Lenny once and for all.

Although Gilgamesh was wary of me—he had come to believe that Lenny was everyone—we went together to see how the Pilgrim brothers were doing.

We found Dottie with the two young warriors, the three locked together in a bizarre sexual configuration. Gilgamesh wanted to incinerate them on the spot, but I stayed his hand. "Let's hear them out," I said.

Skye announced that Dottie was a great person, and Solo said the same thing in other words. They had always liked the same women, he added, which made Dottie laugh. It all seemed so innocent until, without warning, Lenny abruptly appeared as if Dottie's childish laugh had invented him. Brandishing an odd-looking sword, he decapitated the unsuspecting Skye in a single stroke, the tarnished young warrior letting out a heartbreaking cry of surprise and disappointment.

In the next moment Lenny escaped through one of the airshafts, howling with laughter.

Before Lenny could cause any more trouble, I succeeded somehow in blowing Dottie out of the airshaft into endless space, which seemed to herald the monster's disappearance as well.

Unfortunately, Solo Pilgrim, who had pursued Lenny after his brother's murder, also ended up going the same route. The expense had been great, but the immediate danger was apparently over.

So I was in a state of mourning for my lost crew when we landed on what I presumed was the dark side of Lunatha, and

I opened my sealed instructions to find out the nature of my assignment, discovering instead the unforgivable treachery of the authorities on the Star Planet.

My instructions were to turn over ship and surviving crew to the Insidious Emperor and put myself in his service. Someone at home had betrayed us and had used Hank V, the computer—we had been delivered to the innermost fortress of the Insidious Empire (Death Central)—as means to that end.

I tried to take off again, but the magnetic ground of the Death Central landing strip held the ship fast. When, as instructed, I opened the doors to the spaceship (what other options had I?) and let down the ramp, two storm-trooper types came on board to conduct me to the Insidious Emperor. The red carpet was out, which I imagined was someone's idea of irony, and I was treated as a celebrity (the local populace threw flowers) as I made my way through the Palace of Gloom to the Emperor's headquarters.

The Emperor was standing with his back to me when I entered, and I waited with anxious anticipation for him to turn in my direction and acknowledge me.

The surprises did not end with my red carpet reception. The stoop-shouldered Emperor, who embraced me warmly, resembled my long-standing adversary, Linus Poole, who had done some monstrous things on earth before being committed to an institution for the criminally insane. The next unhappy surprise followed almost immediately when the Prime Minister, the emperor's second in command, came out of the inner office to present himself. It was the interminable Lenny himself, Dottie's bad dream, looking as cruel and loathsome as ever.

According to the Emperor, the Star Planet was actually a subsidiary of the Insidious Empire, though the citizenry of that planet for reasons of security remained uninformed of the fact. Some planets were happier not knowing, he said, that their destiny—their sanction to exist—was in another's hands.

In the morning, the Emperor said, after we all had a good night's sleep, he was going to disintegrate the Star Planet while it was in the early stages of its decline. He saw it as an act of kindness, a kind of mass mercy killing. Champagne was passed around, champagne so dry that its taste was spectral, and we drank a toast at his command "to the end of an era." After that I was conducted to a luxurious room, which had every conceivable comfort, and locked in for the night. In a state of despair, I drifted off to sleep.

I woke almost immediately to find myself in the Space Tramp, my crew (all of them alive) standing around my bunk.

I learned that I had had an accident—I had hit my head when we crash-landed—and that we were still in port on the Isle of Dreams, though repairs had been made and we could take off as soon as I gave the order.

The dream, if that's what it was, had been breathtakingly real. It took me awhile to reorient myself. I was not a prisoner behind the space shield of the Insidious Empire. I was in my own ship, my crew still alive, the future open to negotiation.

That's when Gilgamesh, whom we had affectionately named Big Daddy, called my attention to the Viewfinder Monitor which showed a lizard-like creature attacking a young woman in a high-school boiler room. "Shouldn't we look into it?" he asked.

I avoided a direct answer, mumbled something about human decency being a matter of private conscience. Then I got the hell out of there as fast as I could, reprogramming the computer to bypass Lunatha and take us to Disney World on Earth. I was not sure that my decision was in everyone's best interest, but when I told the crew what I had done, I received a standing ovation.

"You are a star again," Marilyn whispered.

twenty-six

Space navigation, when conducted at a rate beyond the speed of light, is an approximate act. We didn't touch down in Disney World, which was our programmed destination, but found ourselves instead on a remote island in the South Atlantic called New Primavera, which apparently had come into being from the volcanic ash of the old. Our fiery arrival from the sky gave us godlike status with the natives at first—all that was required of us was that we bless the crops and insure the harvest—but the longer we stayed, the less enchanted our hosts became with us. When the weather turned bad, we were held responsible as if we had willfully betrayed their trust.

The loss of the Primaverans affection was a disturbing turn. In the best of faith, without fully understanding their language, we strove to become their idea of us (really our idea of their idea), which brought us, for a while, adoration and beads. When our audience began to turn surly and throw rotted vegetables at the spaceship and shoot poison-tipped arrows in our direction, we gradually realized that our show had run its course. It was good times for as long as it lasted, and I wasn't alone in regretting our expulsion.

When we finally got the spaceship in the air again, a flight of spears followed in our wake like a formation of long-tailed birds. We had all gone native during our stay on the island and seemed to have forgotten the rudiments of our space technology. Our talking computer had gone mute on us (Hank would hum or whistle from time to time) and had lost its capacity to navigate. Accident guided us to southern California, chance and miscalculation directed us to the parking lot of a newly constructed mall in the exurban sprawl of greater Los Angeles. As a consequence of our flashy arrival out of the sky, some doomsday religious sect identified us as messengers from God, offering us a mix of devotion and loathing.

We were all a little tired of the god bit, which had been done to death on our remote Atlantic island, so as soon as the spotlight was off, we all went our separate ways, seeking anonymity and new lives. The beads I had brought back from the island turned out to be rare precious stones, and after selling them off and making a few wise investments, I found myself a wealthy man beyond anything I'd ever imagined. When word got out that I was a potential player, movie scripts in wearying profusion found their way on invisible legs to my hotel room. I was suddenly on everyone's list of places to visit.

And so I became a figure in the motion-picture industry again, this time as the CEO of a one-man production company called Black Hole Pictures. I must have read over a hundred scripts before I found two that had something sufficiently important to say to put my name and dollars on the line. The first one, *The Seduction of Lulu's Mother*, based on an incident in my youth—a tragic affair with an older woman—despite hostile reviews, did well with the teen market and won a special prize at Cannes. The second, which dealt with the last decadent days preceding the French Revolution, had even greater critical and commercial success. *The Last Musketeer*, as it's called—you've probably heard of it (no? you will)—has just entered national release. *Musketeer*, which I had a hand in writing, is about the rakish life and times of a French noble of mysterious birth, Maxim A, raised in the country by bookish peasants.

At seventeen—I'm giving you just the basic folderol— our hero leaves home to find his true father and to make his fortune in the world. He takes up with (or is taken up by) a beautiful older woman, the notorious Lady M, a former mistress of the king, who teaches Maxim worldliness, mostly by example, and the pleasures of lovemaking. She also teaches him to use a sword, to seduce a virgin, and to speak an epigram.

When he is sufficiently tutored, she presents Maxim in court as her nephew. The high-spirited Maxim is a great favorite among the women, which gets him in trouble from time to time with vengeance-minded, jealous husbands. In his first duel, he fatally wounds the second most skilled swordsman in Paris, the former Musketeer, Captain Scarf. On his deathbed, Captain Scarf makes Maxim promise that he will look after his wife and child.

To honor his promise, Maxim moves in with Captain Scarf's wife, Antoinette, a noble gesture which alienates Lady M, who swears revenge. While living with Antonette, Maxim takes up with other beautiful women—it is his view of his role—and he is challenged to a record number of duels which earns him in the amplitude of time the reputation of being the most heroic rake in all of France, a distinction that comes with a corresponding number of dangerous enemies and a handful of bereaved widows to comfort.

Meanwhile, the treacherous Lady M conspires with a foppish cabal of royal discontents to disgrace Maxim. She makes the young rake a wager (her renewed sexual favors at stake) that he will be unable to seduce the king's beautiful teenage daughter, who is currently living in a convent in Avignon. Disguised as a monk, the audacious Maxim gets himself installed as a gardener at the convent where the king's daughter, Roxanne, is being schooled to enter the great world as a princess.

One day, Maxim (in his monk disguise) finds Roxanne weeping in the garden, and he brings her a white rose. "I am your friend, child," he tells her. "Your most precious considerations are safe with me." Roxanne confides that convent life is boring as hell and that she misses her lover, the dashing Chevalier de Gras.

Maxim counsels that while she is at the convent she is to think of him as the Chevalier. The princess is moved by the offer and says he is already her best friend (not including the absent Chevalier). In the course of the interview, Maxim falls desperately in love with the charming girl.

Meanwhile, one of Lady M's spies has reported to the king that it is rumored that Maxim has become his daughter's secret lover. If it is true, the king vows, Maxim's next and last assignation will be with Lady Guillotine. The provoked king dispatches one of his aides, the Chevalier de Gras, on a secret mission to the convent to check out the troubling rumors concerning Roxanne's virtue.

Roxanne, who makes her daily confession to Maxim in the garden and has come to love him as he her, confides that her lover, the Chevalier, has sent word that he is coming to visit the convent. What should she do? she asks. "I will look into his heart and see if he is worthy of you," Maxim says.

The mysterious nun with the Mona Lisa smile, who has been observing them from a cloister window, is revealed as the vengeful Lady M in borrowed habit.

Maxim meets the Chevalier de Gras' coach the next night, and he presents himself to his rival as Roxanne's confessor and friend. At first, the Chevalier distrusts the apparent monk, but eventually —a sword fight becomes the occasion of their bonding—Maxim wins him over. A plan is devised between them whereby the Chevalier will go to Roxanne's cell disguised as Maxim (in monk's disguise). At their next meeting in the garden, Maxim tests Roxanne by offering to bring the Chevalier to see her, or not, as she wishes. Roxanne chooses the first option, which disillusions her amorous confessor, who has to turn his hooded face away to disguise his disappointment.

Costumed as a monk, the Chevalier makes his way through the corridors of the convent toward Roxanne's cell. Thinking him the real Maxim, Lady M's spies intercept the hooded figure and attempt to kill him. The Chevalier kills two of his attackers, but does not escape unharmed. Maxim comes on the scene just in time and drives off the remaining assassins, saving his wounded rival's life.

The treacherous Lady M, disguised as Mother Superior, visits Roxanne's cell and whispers in her ear that Maxim is not the monk he appears to be and that he has betrayed her by killing the Chevalier. She comforts the bereaved princess and (this is suggested rather than shown) makes love to her. At Lady M's instigation, Roxanne, armed with a dagger, goes to Maxim's cell to take her revenge. She repeatedly stabs the one sleeping figure in the dark room, then falls to her knees in remorse. She has done the unthinkable: she has killed the man she loves. Hearing her profess her love, Maxim appears from behind a curtain, and after a moment's confusion, Roxanne rushes into his arms.

In the following scene we learn that Maxim is the king's illegitimate son and so Roxanne's half brother.

Her confession signed and sealed, Lady M is brought back to Paris in chains, sentenced to death, and imprisoned in the Bastille. She pretends to repent, weeping and praying, confesses that Maxim is her son, seduces her confessor, kills him, and with the assistance of the Chevalier de Gras, lately in her thrall, escapes from prison.

A masked ball is being given at court—a tradition of the period—to celebrate the princess's return to the royal life. Maxim, newly honored by the king as his son, and officially announced as successor to the throne, dances with a succession of masked beautiful women. A woman, costumed as a black widow spider, petitions him for a dance. As the prince and the spider woman glide about, a poisoned needle on the side of the woman's ring scratches Maxim's palm. In the progress of the dance, the spider-woman, who is of course the treacherous Lady M, inadvertently scratches herself with her poisoned ring—or perhaps, her vengeance satisfied, Lady M decides to follow in Maxim's path. In any event, sweat dotting their foreheads, Maxim and Lady M whirl around and around in ever decreasing speed. The other dancers stop to watch them. Holding each other for support, shivering from the effects of the poison, they prolong their final dance for as long as the fading camera eye permits us to watch them.

Outside the chateau (the scene established in a 180-degree pan) the French Revolution has started, and we glimpse the slaughter, foppish bodies everywhere, aristocratic blood running in the streets.

It had been a personal movie for me, a version of my story in period disguise. In the test screenings, seventy-two percent of the sample audience wanted Maxim to survive and find true love. When I asked the director, a talented journeyman, to make some minor modifications, he threatened to take his name off the picture, so I had no choice but to let him go and reshoot the ending on my own authority. What a pleasure it was to see the world again through the camera's omniscient eye!

*

It was five in the morning when I concluded the above, and I took notice again of the sly, skeptical faces observing me. "My assignment," I told Wilfred Cog, who appeared the most sympathetic of my captors, "was to make movies."

"I see," said Wilfred Cog who was unfailingly polite, "but there must be something more."

"Yes," I said. "I was having dinner with a writer-director who had pitched a high-concept picture to me, concerning a failed stand-up comic who has a second career in the afterlife, when I got up to make a phone call to a former wife at the moment your people were paging a man you had never seen before called Philip Levy."

But they knew all that and had no interest in hearing what came next.

After tying my hands behind me and my feet to one another, my captors, who were in an irritable mood, went off to another room to confer. Wilfred Cog did not return. One of his assistants, Summerfield, I believe, held me while the other, Hermann, poured most of a fifth of whiskey down my throat. What awaited me, I remembered thinking before I lost consciousness, was a one-way trip to the river of no return.

twenty-seven

I woke up the next morning, hungover, in an unfamiliar hotel room, a smoking gun at the foot of my bed, a dead body lying in the center of the room like its own tracing. I had been awakened by a pounding on the door and an obvious police presence shouting, "Open up."

As I was an innocent man caught in a maelstrom of misunderstanding, I climbed out of bed and opened the door. The two policemen seemed hellbent on arresting me, when I pointed out that a man who had something to hide wouldn't have admitted them.

"Mr. Bedford, the criminal mind will go to any length to disguise the nature of its crimes," said the cop who had introduced himself as Sergeant Black.

My name wasn't Bedford and had never been. I showed them my wallet, which had Max Million's name on the identification card.

The two policeman, who were never less than polite, checked the information they had been given from headquarters and discovered they were one smudged digit off on the room number. In their zealousness, they had forced their way into the wrong hotel room and arrested a man who was not in their jurisdiction. Since this was not their case, not at the moment, they removed my handcuffs and gave me ten minutes to get my life in order.

I dressed in the dead man's clothes—nothing else was available—and hurried out of the hotel room, which was on the 29th floor. How did I get here? I wondered. It was not a question I often asked myself. Crisis had deepened me in a myriad of barely perceptible ways.

My plan was to go to my hotel room at the Algonquin, take a hot shower, change my clothes, call my New York office and perhaps even a lawyer, but as I stepped out of the elevator, I saw one of the two men who had kidnapped me the day before.

I slipped back into the elevator, bumping into (in both senses) a familiar, slightly tarnished semi-beautiful blonde woman getting in at the same time.

There's a man out there trying to kill me, I said smiling, hoping it didn't sound as crazy to her as it did to me.

I wouldn't be at all surprised, Mr. Levy, she said. Your picture's on the front page of almost every newspaper in America.

The woman, for her own reasons which were yet to make themselves known, offered to hide me in her room until the worst of the heat was off.

Her room turned out to be on the 30th Floor just above my former room, an odd coincidence which made me distrustful.

When Maria Carlyle, which was the name she gave me, was out on an errand, I called my office to explain my absence and was told by my own secretary that I couldn't possibly be Max Million since the real Max Million happened to be working at his desk as we spoke.

The other man is an imposter, I told her. The reason I'm not in the office, Jane, is that I'd been kidnapped by people who had mistaken me for a spy and then refused to recognize their mistake in my regard, and so to cover themselves got me drunk and framed me for a murder.

She hung up or we were cut off from another source. Before I could call back, I heard Sergeant Black's voice in the hall and footsteps toward or away. What to do—that persistent question. I shaved myself with a woman's tiny razor, then dressed myself in Maria Carlyle's clothes and put on one of her blonde wigs.

The high heels got to me—I had never worn heels before—and my ankles began to wobble in a telltale way as I walked through the lobby to the Grill Room, where lunch was being served, at the very moment someone coming out of the restaurant was assassinated with a knife.

In the ensuing confusion, the blood-stained knife ended up in my left hand.

There were screams, someone pointing a finger at me, the real murderer, the sociopath Summerfield, slipping out the door while attention focused itself on the odd-looking woman with the blood-stained knife.

In the commotion, someone knocked off my wig, which created a gasp of uncomfortable surprise. I punched a man trying to hold on to me and got out the door just in time to see Summerfield, who had a face like a barber's razor, get into one of the cabs that hang around outside the hotel.

Short of other options, I jumped into the next cab and instructed the driver the way they do in movies to follow the cab just ahead. Out of the side of my eye, I noticed Maria Carlyle standing in front of the hotel, talking to Wilfred Cog himself.

As we pursued the cab in front, our cab was being followed in turn by an unmarked (I assumed) police car. We were in Yonkers somewhere when the lead cab, aware of our shadow, made a series of abrupt unexpected turns.

Too late to make the second of two sharp sudden turns, my cab crashed into a telephone pole.

Six months later, I woke in a hospital bed with no memory of a past. I woke from my dream on a Tuesday at 4:10 in the afternoon in an unfamiliar white room as if I had just been torn from the womb. The afternoon nurse, a light-skinned black woman, addressed me as a Mr. Willow. "Any discomfort, Mr. Willow?" she asked.

"Head," I heard myself say, unable to locate a second word to follow the first. In truth, I had what felt like a toothache at the back of my head.

At five o'clock, a fatuous doctor with the name tag Bedford on his whites came by to joke about my being again among the living, referring to me, as had the nurse, as Mr. Willow.

During the night, the older man in the bed next to me, a man of brooding silences, was removed forcibly by two men in stocking feet.

*

The next day I had a visitor, an almost beautiful semi-blonde woman I had only the dimmest recollection of having seen before. Her manner toward me suggested long-term intimacy. "Is there anything I can do for you, darling?" she asked, sitting on the side of the bed.

"Get me out of here," I said.

The woman stood up as if I had pushed her away. "Don't be impatient, Chance," she said, pacing, her back to me. "Dr. Bedford said you're making wonderful progress. Besides when you get out, the police will want to talk to you." I did ask one question: Why should the police want to talk to me? "Oh the usual reasons," she said, telling me nothing, "loose ends that needed to be tied together in cases like this. Loose ends. You know, loose ends," as if it were all too obvious for words. She called me Chance, which was probably a nickname, long or short for something else.

The next night, perhaps in a dream, I heard two men whispering behind a wall. One said, "I think he's only pretending not to remember." The other whispered in return, "Before it's over, Bill, we'll have to exterminate them all."

The almost young, almost beautiful woman, whose behavior implied long-term intimacy, who as it turned out was someone I once knew under another name, returned two days later with a set of neatly pressed doctors' whites in an an unmarked shopping bag. We passed amused semi-smiles back and forth as we walked down the long corridor of the sinister hospital to the front door, which was guarded by two armed men in uniform. I couldn't get over the feeling that someone behind or above was watching our every move.

twenty-eight

The stencilled name on my uniform was Dr. Levy, which struck a remote chord of recognition. Was it possible that I was leaving the hospital actually disguised as myself? Even after this almost beautiful woman and I escaped together in her metallic blue Dodge Polaris, I had no clear idea of how I should behave toward her, what was expected and what was not.

My rescuer took me to a nondescript white cottage in the country, an hour's drive from the hospital, the interior generically furnished in standard good taste. In one of the upstairs bedrooms there was a closet full of men's clothes in my size of a style so fashionably anonymous they might have been tailor-made for an amnesiac.

"This was the best I could do on short notice, Chance," she said, holding out a double-breasted blazer for me to try on. It all happened so quickly, the escape from the hospital, the drive to the country, the room by room tour of the cottage which was to be my temporary home, the not-quite-right multicourse gourmet dinner the woman prepared for me, that none of it fully registered as experience. It was as if I were watching the life of someone else, someone like myself, on the bigger-than-life screen of a movie theater.

When the woman announced after dinner that she had to get back to the city, I asked when I would see her again, beginning to miss her before she was gone. As soon as it's safe to return, she said, working out a phone signal (one ring and then an immediate call back) so I would know whether to answer when the phone rang. In my ignorance it seemed an excessive precaution.

In her absence, I snooped around, trying to find out who she was and who I was and what we might be to each other. On a kitchen table, I discovered a picture postcard (a reproduction of the Mona Lisa) sent from Paris to a Ms. Miriam Hart, a name that struck only the most distant echo of familiarity.

It was the usual tourist message—saw this and that, loving Paris, undaunted by the drizzle and the weakness of the dollar. So usual, that I wondered if there weren't some kind of coded message behind the traditional banalities. The card was signed with the initial "W".

In the den, there was a picture of the two of us cutting into a wedding cake with the same knife. The caption underneath read "Chance and Miriam: Is this only the beginning?"

Exhaustion reached the brain or the heart, and I collapsed on one of the living room couches.

A sudden noise woke me. I was immediately aware that someone else was in the house, in an adjoining room, rooting around in an impatient heat. Whoever it was must have already been through the living room, which was the first room you enter, and had not noticed the sleeping figure hunkered down on the black corduroy couch.

When the phone rang, the intruder answered from the kitchen. "Don't call again," an unplaceably familiar voice with a faint German accent rasped. "I'll be in touch after the cottage is torched."

When I heard the intruder go upstairs, I got off the couch and slipped outside into the steely night air. My first impulse was to get away, and with that in mind, I got into the black Mercedes parked 50 yards or so down the road. There was no key in the ignition which precluded my immediate escape so I hid myself in the back, a wrench in my right hand, waiting for the intruder, whose name I seemed to remember as Wilfred Cog, to come for his car.

I fell asleep waiting, woke with a start the moment the engine turned over with an expensive purr. The wrench was under me and to get it I had to raise my legs without calling attention to myself. As Cog lit a cigarette, I brought down the wrench on the back of his head, an awkward glancing blow. Cursing in an unknown language, Cog turned toward me with a gun in his hand, but I got a better swing at him the second time, leaving him slumped like an inflated doll against the door.

I rolled the body out of the car and was going through his pockets, when I noticed that a fire had started in one of the upstairs rooms of the cottage. I left Cog, assuming he was dead, in the dim hope of saving the cottage, arriving too late— a few buckets of water inadequate to the task—the blaze raging out of control.

After calling the fire department, I went back to the black Mercedes, which was not where it had been, having vanished in my absence like a magician's trick.

Lying on my belly in the field, I watched the flames and the cottage decline together in luminous partnership. When the fire was finally out and the trucks gone, I went back inside the ruined cottage and called the almost young, almost beautiful woman, who may or may not be Miriam Hart from the melted kitchen phone still hot to the touch. I reported what had happened, giving her a description of the intruder. She was her usual cryptic self on the phone, advising me not to leave the house and not to let anyone in, saying she would be there as fast as humanly possible.

I was going through the rubble looking for clarifying detail when I heard several cars drive up. Looking out from the charred remains of the cottage, I had the impression the field was on fire. What I saw were the flashing turrets of five perhaps six police cars.

WILLOW, COME OUT WITH YOUR HANDS ABOVE YOUR HEAD, a voice blared. THIS IS SERGEANT BLACK REPEAT SERGEANT BLACK SPEAKING.

Before I could decide on a course of action, bullets flew through the shattered house like a plague of locusts. I took refuge in a crawl space behind the stairs, waiting for the gunfire to exhaust itself.

Periodically, the loudspeaker announcement returned, threatening and cajoling, having it both ways, all ways, offering brief respite before the indiscriminate shooting resumed.

When the rubble caught fire from the blast of what may have been a hand grenade, I crawled out an opening in a kitchen wall into a connecting garage that had somehow survived the blaze. Finding a moped in the garage, I drove off on it into the dense backwoods as if, which was contrary to semi-remembered fact, I had been riding one all my life.

Two police cars came after me, but the woods resisted their entrance, and the cops were forced to pursue on foot. And then, looking over my shoulder, I crashed into a tree stump. The fall, as falls will, jogged loose much of my buried memory (like seeing the beginning of a movie when you already know the outcome), and so I knew who I was again as I stumbled through the dense brush away from unseen pursuers. I was Max Million (called Fret when I was young), one of the top independent producers on the scene, a man with a gift for the semi-sincere persuasive image, a man who had forsaken his own planet to redeem his career and had returned to Hollywood to see his name once again above the title, his lost name, his forgotten self.

On the other side of the woods, I came to a dirt road which led to Wilfred Cog's country estate, the place to which I had been abducted at the beginning of this adventure. In fact, Cog's black Mercedes, which I now regretted not driving off in when I had the chance, was parked in one of the five adjoining carports. Of the other cars parked out front, there were three other Mercedes, each of a different color, and a familiar metallic blue Dodge Polaris—the car I had been taken in by Miriam Hart when we escaped from the sinister hospital.

I reconnoitered around the house, peering into windows to get the lay of things. There was a painting of the young Adolph Hitler prominently displayed on a black velvet wall with the embroidered caption "Ich bin New Yorker" underneath. Wilfred Cog, wearing a bandage around his head the size and scope of a turban, was packing the viscera of an assassin's rifle inside an attache case, while his aides, Summerfield and Hermann, were tying Miriam Hart (aka Maria Carlyle) to a chair. There were several men around in black uniforms wearing swastika armbands. When I leave, Cog was saying, I want Ms. Carlyle, who has betrayed our cause, and the Jew Levy, who is probing about on the grounds somewhere, to know what it is to die a slow and ignominious death. After those who would defy us are worm meat,

Hermann, torch anything in the house that might connect us with the assassination.

At that moment, the police pursuing me on foot arrived at Cog's estate, just as Cog, carrying his ominous attache case, got into his car and drove off. One of Cog's men, the notorious Summerfield, had opened fire on the police, who were answering fire with fire, creating sufficient diversion for me to climb in through a window, disable Hermann in an extended fight which changed complexion several times before its happy conclusion, and free Miriam/Maria using Hermann's cigarette lighter to burn through her ropes.

Miriam, it appeared—I had only her own word to go on—was a double (perhaps triple) agent working for the U.S. government, which seemed to explain the vagaries of her behavior toward me, including a marriage in name only to a former amnesiac identity named Chance. She had turned to government service in despair after my reported death—really Marco's death—behind the iron curtain. When she ran into me in the elevator of the Plaza she had been working (on assignment from the government) for Wilfred Cog. After that, while seeming to do her job (for all her employers), she did what she could to keep Cog and his people (and the various forces aligned against Cog) from killing me. And after a while, resist as she might, the old feelings returned.

As before, as always, there was no time to lose, though personal matters—love perhaps (there was barely time for our second first kiss)—tended to slow things down. I slipped out of the house unnoticed and into Miriam's car and drove around the back where Miriam, as arranged, was waiting for me. As she was getting into the passenger side, a random bullet, probably from one of the team of police, hit her in the most circumstantial way, glancing off the door of the car and into her skull.

I carried Miriam out of the car and back toward the house. The fighting had mostly stopped—occasional shots here and there echoed like afterthoughts.

As I was carrying Miriam into the house, a second group of police arrived led by the indefatigable Sergeant Black. I put her down gently on the orange and ivory Ming Dynasty rug in the front room, refusing to believe, having cut myself off from believing, that Miriam (whom I had known in high school as Sassy and had loved almost forever) was already dead.

Sergeant Black was standing over me. A lot of people have been looking for you, Willow, he said.

I woke with my head in Sassy's lap, but that was another dream.

The police doctor came in and, after examining Sassy, placed a sheet over the body. "She won't be running any more stoplights," he said.

Black played with his moustache. "I admit we've made a few mistakes along the way, Willow," he said. "I freely admit to some misapprehensions, but I think you'll be impressed to know that we've got Wilfred Cog in custody, picked him up not five miles from here. I guess that makes you a free man."

I lingered a moment. I had been too long on the wrong end of the fox hunt to give up my role of injured innocence without second thoughts. Walking toward the door, I had an odd premonition (a part of the puzzle was still missing), and I turned back. And just in time. I discovered a gun pointed at what had been my back, cocked, primed to fire. There was also a gun in my own hand, the one cancelling out the other.

"Don't you trust anyone?" said the sergeant.

The standoff lasted five minutes, perhaps ten, at which point (and for reasons which soon may become clear) Sgt. Black withdrew his gun. In the next moment, a man identified as Wilfred Cog was brought into the house by two government agents for questioning.

I was astonished. This Wilfred Cog was several inches shorter and perhaps five years younger than the Wilfred Cog who had tried to kill me. "This is the wrong man," I said.

The government agent in charge, a Philip Levy, assured me that the man in his custody was indeed the real Wilfred Cog, hotshot lawyer, defender of lost causes, a man who would do anything for a headline. The real Wilfred Cog, who was the wrong man in my perception alone, had agreed to turn over his co-conspirators, Levy reported, in exchange for his freedom.

Someone had to stop the impending assassination and the senseless killing that would flow from it. I took advantage of the general confusion and rushed out of the house and down the road to Sassy's metallic blue Dodge Polaris, taking off after the dangerous imposter with the assassin's rifle in his attache case. An unmarked government car took pursuit, Philip Levy at the wheel, seeking, as were we all, some point of clarity. The wrong (though authentic) Wilfred Cog, who was turning state's evidence, had identified me as an accomplice. Once again I was a wanted man.

There was no point of clarity down the road, merely the mechanism of pursuit and empty discovery. There were more chases to come in this case, more instances of mistaken identity, more murders, more delusory solutions to murder, more willful destruction of property, more questions without answers, more neo-Nazis rising from the ashes, more enigmatic assassins, more almost young, almost beautiful women (who may or may not be spies), more betrayal, more lost love. All the wrong people (only the wrong people) would be caught and punished, the inevitable happy ending a deceptive waystation, an accommodating illusion to permit us to go on to more of the same: more deaths, more fast automobiles, more dimwitted spying, more incomprehensible secrets. And your man, myself, the fugitive Willow, the Hollywood producer Max Million, the teenager Fret, was caught up in this feverish continuum, this unshakable dream, misperceived and disbelieved, wanting only to be free of my pursuers, and to prove my innocence, and to make movies, and to live the good life, all of which among the wisdom disappointment had to offer was implicitly promised from the beginning, was dangled before me, given and taken away and which, while in flight from the furies of misguided justice, I continue to pursue as if the pursuit of false hope were itself the last good thing—the only reward.

twenty-nine

One night, after eluding a black florist's van that had pursued me across three states, I woke up in my car at the side of the road and refocused on the one thing my amnesia had for the longest time persisted in keeping from me—Marisan, my inamorata, was waiting for me (or had been) at the Paradise Hotel in New York City. There was not a moment to waste.

I drove straight through to New York without food or sleep—my watch had stopped sometime back at five after eleven so I have no way of accounting the duration of the trip—and when I finally reached the Paradise Hotel, I was at some hallucinatory stage beyond exhaustion. When I got inside the hotel—the night clerk dozing at his post, his snores like some industrial hum—I could barely stand upright. I struggled to remember the number of the room. Unsequenced numbers floated randomly in my head. The room, if resurrected memory could be trusted, was on the third or fourth floor. I opened a few doors, staring into unfamiliar dark rooms, the secret lives of strangers revealing themselves to me. Determination overrode embarrassment. Although years, perhaps even decades, had passed since I left our hotel room to buy Marisan an egg salad sandwich on whole wheat, I had to believe, even as I doubted myself, that she was still waiting for me.

I was in a state of near collapse when I found the room—it was 4B and I recognized it immediately, the same airless cave in which our brief idyll had magically played itself out. I pushed open the door, which was ajar, and noticed a woman in the bed, only her head showing from under the crumpled sheet.

She was virtually unrecognizable, had lost considerable weight, though all that mattered at the moment was that she was there and still alive. Her eyes blinked open. "You're late," she said in a frail voice, sitting up in bed. I stumbled toward her holding out the apple I had brought her (from a fruit stand in South Carolina), in lieu of the sandwich I had failed to get.

I got out of my sweat-soaked clothes and waited for her to eat the apple before I embraced her. "My husband came for me about six months ago," she said, "but I told him I was waiting for you and couldn't leave."

I told her about being shot in the head and losing my memory and going back to San Francisco (and another time to Los Angeles) to look for her twice in the wrong place, and opening an office as a private eye and being hired by a sinister psychiatrist to follow his sleepwalking wife, and then rescuing the wife, a former FBI agent named Veronika Kay, and then escaping with her to Seattle, and then solving a series of daring daylight jewel robberies which were committed by a woman with a rare disease that had rendered her colorless, and then getting involved in the solution of some ugly obsessive crimes, which made me close to crazy myself, and then ending up in a mental institution, not because I was crazy, but because I had become an undercover agent for a counterintelligence organization, which led me to Russia during the last days of the cold war, and then, after a few years on a planet in another galaxy, being kidnapped (by mistake) by renegade government agents turning me into the perpetual fugitive you see before you, this just a few weeks after I had made a comeback in Hollywood, completing the second of two independent, midbudget major motion pictures, and all that time I was trying to remember who you were and the name of the hotel to which I was supposed to return.

"I had my lapses too,"she said. "I fell in love with someone else for a short time, but my voices, which returned to me after you went out the door, told me you would return and so I waited."

She was almost fleshless, and when I lifted her from the bed, she seemed to have no more weight than a photographic image. I would have been content merely to hold her, but she

171

wrapped her legs around me, and we mingled like particles of dust, like crossing winds, our bones seeming to merge inside the dust of our frailty, as we made love in a kind of slow motion, pain visiting pain. After I came (and she too, one dusty whisper answering another), we stayed locked together, moving so slowly we seemed not to be moving at all.

We stayed together another three days, which was how long she lived.

"Please turn on the light," she said, repeating her request several times. Of course, the light was already on. "I want to see your face." Those were her last words.

I continued to talk to Marisan even after she was dead, telling her about my half-brother, Marco, and my falling-down sickness, and about Marco's wife, Miriam, who had been a childhood sweetheart called Sassy, and how I had estranged myself from Miriam irrevocably by pretending to be my own brother, who was dead, and in the process—it was in the nature of self-betrayal—I had lost myself as well.

There was no time to complete the story. The appearance of a black florist's van parked illegally across the street, which I picked up on from the room's one soot-scarred window, caused me to flee the hotel by escaping through a bathroom window on the second floor.

When I fell asleep at the wheel of my car doing fifty-five on some scenic highway, I dreamed of the two of us flying together on a ghostly airline, the plane without passengers except for a man without a face and Marisan, beautiful as ever, our hands connected secretively under a blanket—the stewardess serving egg salad sandwiches to the empty seats around us—an unfamiliar rendition of "Stand By Me" by The Grateful Dead on the soundtrack, the music disturbing and unforgettable. For a moment I knew who I was, remembered my deepest most personal secrets, and then when I turned my head to escape the clamor of a police siren, it was all hopelessly lost—it was like water spilling from my ear—forever.